BRING ME
THE HEAD OF
MR. BOOTS

D0834676

CHARLES
HOLDEFER

Sagging
Meniscus

Thanks to Eric Engdahl and Kay Burnett.

© 2019 by Charles Holdefer

All Rights Reserved.

Printed in Great Britain and the United States of America.
Set in Mrs Eaves XL with LaTeX.

ISBN: 978-1-944697-79-2 (paperback)
ISBN: 978-1-944697-90-7 (ebook)
Library of Congress Control Number: 2019942815

Sagging Meniscus Press
www.saggingmeniscus.com

"You can fool some of the people all of the time, and all of the people some of the time, but you can't fool all of the people all of the time."

—Abraham Lincoln*

*Lincoln never said this, according to some historians, who assert that people have been fooled.

BRING ME THE HEAD OF MR. BOOTS

Contents

GIGS

Serena

"IF ANYBODY ASKS QUESTIONS, just pretend you're lost, right? It's a big house, it's easy to get lost. But wherever you go, plant a monitor. Keep an eye out. You can always say you were looking for a bathroom."

Erich opened a door and discovered an office. No time to linger—he walked straight to the desk and stuck the monitor behind one of its supporting legs and then walked out, soundlessly closing the door behind him.

The next room was, well, a bathroom. He gave it a quick inspection. The medicine cabinet was almost empty, so clearly this wasn't Mr. Plutov's main bathroom where he went about his everyday needs. (Imagine the FBI agents who *listen* to this stuff, Erich thought. What a job!) He stuck a monitor behind the toilet and left quickly.

From downstairs came the sound of tinkling music, shouts. At least he'd put those awful kids behind him. As part of today's entertainment, Erich had started by making balloon animals in front of an enormous birthday cake. Pink frosting letters declared HAPPY BIRTHDAY VIKTOR! The cake looked big enough for a stripper to jump out of, but it wasn't that kind of party. The children cawed and crowed while Erich's hands busily twisted and turned the squeaky rubber. A pug-nosed, puffy-faced kid in the front row scrolled down a smart phone, ignoring him.

"How about this?" Erich said. "A doggie!"

The kid looked up. "You suck," he said.

All the children laughed.

This was his introduction to Viktor. Erich smiled gamely while a silent woman with jet-black hair moved among the group and refilled paper cups with juice. He supposed she was a live-in nanny. Perhaps Guatemalan? Mayan? Lots of these lakefront places in Wilmette had live-ins.

He stretched the rubber of another balloon, blew it up and worked it into sausage-like segments, wrestling them into form. He held it out. "Look—a giraffe!" With startling swiftness, Viktor seized a plastic fork from a row of utensils and lunged. *Pop!* went the giraffe.

Children screamed in delight.

Now Erich proceeded down the hallway, fingering the monitors in his pocket. He'd never seen anything like them. They were stacked on each other. You peeled one off the top and reapplied the sticky side to a surface out of the line of vision. Like one of those little supermarket labels you found on pieces of fruit, it was easy to move around. But it was silica-based, transparent, and thus blended in with the surface. Even if you knew where to look, you could stare at it and easily miss it. In an eerie way it reminded him of those weird see-through fish he'd marveled at when he was a kid visiting the Shedd Aquarium. Its flesh and bones were well-nigh invisible, in a certain light, as the creature flitted through the water. All you could see was its sly eye.

"You do magic shows," said Agent Heffernan, a petite woman with spiky hair. "You ought to be able to manipulate these little things. Why, they're scarcely bigger than dimes."

Such was the naïveté of a lay person. While Erich took pride in his sleight of hand abilities and was somewhat vain about his better moves (kiddie shows and balloon animals were strictly money-making expedients or unfortunate obligations when the FBI had him by the balls), most people didn't appreciate the sheer difficulty of truly artful manipulation. Practically speaking, a very small object could be harder to handle than something bigger. A dime was more trouble than a quarter or a half dollar. You had to get a grip. And as for handling people—well, sometimes kids were the toughest audience of all, with undeveloped social reflexes, turning savage on a whim. Adults were more obliging when you needed a sucker.

He opened another door and was startled to see a woman sitting on the edge of a bed, half-dressed, lifting a bottle to her mouth. She froze, the bottle in mid-air. "Sorry," he blurted, and closed the door.

"Hey," she yelled. "*Get back here!*"

Slowly he re-opened the door. He remained behind the threshold. "Excuse me. I was just looking for a bathroom."

"Who are you? Come here, I can't see you."

Gingerly Erich stepped into the room. She looked him over. She appeared puzzled but not particularly concerned by his presence. She was wearing some kind of legless gray jumpsuit with a shawl hanging off her shoulders.

"We got bathrooms downstairs," she said, resting the bottle on her bare knee. "What are you really up to? Who *are* you?"

"I didn't know. Sorry. I'm here for the party. I'm Ambrose the Amazing." She frowned and Erich added, "the entertainment?"

She screwed up her eyes and then seemed to remember. "Oh yeah. Yelena recommended you. Well, there's a party up here, too." She took a swig. "All right, magic man. Get your ass over here. Entertain me."

Erich emitted a nervous laugh but didn't budge. He stared at a spot slightly above her head because if he didn't, his gaze went to an exposed shoulder or to her bare legs. "I'm afraid I have a previous engagement," he said. "It's a two-part show? I do the Orbit Count-Down and balloon animals, and then there's an intermission so they can have their cake, and then I come back for Tricky Science, which is not only entertaining but educational?"

As he said this, he experienced a twinge of worry about Boots, the rabbit that he'd left with his travel gear. Boots was a borrowed rabbit and Erich had parked him with his kit in the kitchen. It was important to keep him hydrated.

She took another swig. "I'm paying you. Or not. So come here, Ambrose." She pointed to a water glass on the dresser. "You can use that. Join the party."

Erich stepped closer but didn't take the glass. "No, I really can't."

"Then get the fuck out of my house, dickwad!"

He didn't move. "I don't mean to be unfriendly, don't take it that way. I just can't. I'm in recovery. Swore off drinking and other substances two years ago. Sobriety has made a huge difference in my life. That's all I'm saying."

"Oh my." She pressed her lips together. "You're one of those. Yay for you." She lifted the bottle in the air, then brought it to her lips.

"Everyone is different. But everyone deserves happiness."

Erich meant these words though they weren't his own. Erich's A.A. sponsor, Fred Cunningham, a fat wheezing redfaced man who'd survived a train wreck of a life, had told him exactly the same thing. Fred had been there for him. Fred had also said that unexpected opportunities would arise with other people, chances to reach out.

Erich noticed that he'd crossed his arms while speaking so now he uncrossed them, because he didn't want to appear judgmental.

"All right, then," she said, holding out the bottle. "Take it away. Do me a favor."

He hadn't expected this reaction. But old Fred wouldn't miss this opportunity, he would try to help. Erich extended his hand, and suddenly she pulled back the bottle and grasped his fingers with her other hand. She tugged him toward her. "Well, you'll have to find another way to amaze me."

4

"But—"

She pulled again and he was obliged to pivot to one side to avoid falling onto her: he sat with a thump next to her on the edge of the bed. He looked at her bare legs and then at the bedroom door, which was still open. He was no longer thinking of Fred Cunningham.

She laughed and leaned back, showing more leg.

"You sure?" he said.

"Oh. Did you swear this off, too?"

Agent Heffernan wanted him to explore Plutov's house as much as he could. *Make the most of your time there,* she'd said. But this wasn't what Heffernan intended. Erich had his own doubts, too.

"Well, you know," he replied. "Maybe I've just seen too many movies where some employee fools around and then gets the shit kicked out of him when the husband finds out afterward. That kind of thing?"

"This isn't some movie, Ambrose." She took a swig and lifted a foot in the air, wiggling her toes.

"That's my last name. My first name is Erich."

"Oh by all means, let's introduce ourselves!" She chuckled and lifted her other foot, wiggling. "I'm Serena. Just a small-town girl, really. I used to work at the Dairy Queen. Did you ever ride your bike up to my window for an ice-cream cone?"

Suddenly she sprang to her feet and moved unsteadily to the bedroom door, swinging it closed with a bang. When she turned, her lip curled. "You see, in the movies, the husband actually cares. You have to *care* to kick the shit out of somebody. That's how it works. So don't worry. This man doesn't even care enough to come to his son's birthday party."

She put the bottle on the dresser and began to fiddle with the shawl around her shoulders. Erich realized that it was some kind of a cape. She pointed to the bed. "Throw me my hatty thing."

He noticed a slick black piece of material and tossed it over. When she pulled it on, with its pointed ears and eye slots, he understood. "Viktor likes Batman," she said. "This is a surprise. I'm part of the entertainment, too."

"Nice."

He wasn't being sarcastic, in fact she looked sleek and sexy in her outfit, but somehow his compliment affected her negatively, her shoulders hunched, as if she were suddenly self-conscious. Or maybe she hadn't even heard him, and she was thinking of something else. Perhaps listening to a voice in her head. She reached for the bottle and walked over to a potted plant. She emptied the remaining contents into the plant, and then rested the bottle on the window sill.

"You're right," she told him. "This is stupid. Never mind what I said. I don't mean what I do. How could I? But I'm just so tired and there's so much going on. I need ten minutes to get it together. A little nap. I haven't slept much lately. But I don't want to miss the party."

She returned to the bed and lay on her side, her back to him.

"Don't go yet," she said to the wall. "You don't have to talk and I'd rather you didn't, to tell the truth, but when someone's around I don't have to hear what I'm thinking. Know what I mean? Maybe you could just stay next to me? It doesn't take so much not to be alone. Give me ten minutes. Don't touch me. Don't try anything funny. Just stay. That's not asking so much, is it?"

Her form on the bedspread was small and still, and the room was full of sadness.

"Okay." Erich slipped down beside her, adjusted his pillow, and listened to her steady breathing.

Bad Magician

AFTER FIVE MINUTES, she turned around and faced him. He thought that she was going to speak. Her lips moved slightly, as if asking for something. But there were no words. He watched her mouth, and then he wanted her mouth and he leaned toward her and kissed her on the lips. Was that what she was asking? She kissed him back and lifted a hand to squeeze his shoulder. Her lips were wonderfully soft as he tasted them and then he slid his arm across her arm. Soon they were tugging at each other's clothes. What ensued was not graceful—Erich's sleeve got stuck, partly pulled off backward, and helping Serena out of the jumpsuit was a struggle—but it wasn't unsatisfactory, either. Quite the opposite. The resistance of clothes as they tried to get free added a sense of urgency, fanning their excitement. The fact that she kept on her Batman hat during the act was a distracting detail but he incorporated it into moment. It took him to a new mental place. Once joined, they moved quickly, convulsively; when she let out a shuddering groan it triggered the same in Erich only seconds afterward. Then they were still.

Another minute passed, in silence, and just when he wondered if she was dozing off, she stirred and disentangled herself. "Excuse me." She hopped off the bed and opened a door at the other end of the room. He heard water running in the sink.

Erich sat on the edge of the bed and threaded first one leg, then the other, back into his pants. He looked over his shoulder and when he saw that he was still alone, he reached into his pocket and peeled off a silica monitor and stuck it under the edge of the night table beside the bed. He stood and tucked in his shirt.

She returned, without her hat, her hair mussed, dabbing her face with a towel. "Well," she said. "You're one bad magician."

Erich smiled. "I was hoping you'd say amazing. Stupendous. Unbelievable."

"Let's move it along, Ambrose. You've got to perform."

He pressed his hands together. "Well—sure." He started for the door.

Breakfast at Thurston's

ERICH DIDN'T CONSIDER HIMSELF a snitch. But sometimes it was necessary to mix with some pretty unsavory characters, because the law obliged him to do so. Actually, the law included some pretty unsavory characters. He would've preferred to have nothing to do with the whole crowd.

"I'm not looking for trouble," he'd told Agent Heffernan.

"You've already found it," she'd replied. "The question is, are you going to get out of it? Do you want to help yourself?"

A presumptuous question, made worse by the setting. She'd approached him at Thurston's Diner. Erich sat at the counter, eating eggs and bacon and a big lump of feta cheese. (This wasn't on the menu but one morning he'd spotted an employee eating this dish; he'd said, "Give me one of those"—and *damn*, it was good! It had been his favorite breakfast ever since.) He liked coming to Thurston's. Bacon and eggs and a big lump of feta cheese were an indulgence he could afford. More than an indulgence, really: it would be no exaggeration to say this breakfast was one of the steady, true things in life, when he thought about it—the stress of a career, the regret of a broken marriage, the struggle to face a world without a chemical crutch or the comfort of illusions—what did any of that mean, now, why should he let the past hurt him? Why not just *let it all go*, and focus on simple and beautiful things on this earth like his favorite breakfast and a cup of strong coffee and sunlight streaming through the plate-glass windows. The peace. In its way, Thurston's was a sanctuary. *Simplify*, he'd repeated to himself. *Simplify*. He could do that at Thurston's.

The first time he'd spoken to Agent Heffernan was at FBI regional headquarters on Roosevelt Road. He'd never been inside the federal building before, though for his day job he'd delivered arugula and heirloom tomatoes to restaurants in nearby neighborhoods. He and Agent Heffernan sat in a drab office and went over the same old questions about Mrs. Kubek and her death. He'd already answered these questions a dozen times. Erich was facing serious charges but Heffernan told him that she could make them go away, if he was helpful. "I *am* helpful," he insisted. "I'm telling you everything I know. I don't have a magic wand. You do."

"Don't fool yourself."

They met two more times at her office, and then she stopped calling him. It had been three weeks since they'd spoken. Erich hoped that the FBI had lost interest in him, that somehow he'd slipped through a crack.

Then, a sunny Tuesday morning, as he sat eating his eggs and bacon with a big lump of feta cheese, suddenly Agent Heffernan was sitting at the counter beside him, ordering French toast from the waitress.

So now you're following me! Erich thought. Snooping in my haunts. It felt unnerving and invasive. He'd discovered a snake in *his* diner.

"The thing is," Agent Heffernan said, as if answering a question he hadn't posed, "people think it's easy for us to get warrants and go wherever we want. But it's not. Not as easy as they believe. Judges have to sign off and they have their own ideas and time limits and they're always protecting their career. Procedures, Erich. Exhausting. So where does that leave us? Sometimes a private individual undertakes actions that can provide useful information. Because of circumstances, this information can't be used in court. Fair enough. We respect the law. But sometimes this information leads to other information that *can* be used in court. We respect the law, things get done, everyone wins."

"Uh huh," said Erich. "So. . .if I'm a private individual, what are my actions? In what circumstances?"

"You will be invited to perform at a children's birthday party in Wilmette. Accept the offer. You'll get a good fee. These people have money."

"So what do I do?"

Agent Heffernan stirred creamer in her coffee.

"Some people are very cautious. They won't let strangers into their home. But in order to please their child, they'll make an exception. This is where they're soft. Kids like magic shows."

"Why would they choose me? I haven't done children's shows in years. I'm not on that circuit. I already told you. I'm a close-up performer."

The waitress put down a plate of French toast. "Syrup with that?" she asked.

"Honey, please," said Agent Heffernan.

The waitress came back with a squeezy-bear.

"Lovely," she said. Then she turned to Erich. "They'll choose you because you'll come very highly recommended."

Arrangement with the Dead

THE TROUBLE HAD STARTED after old Mrs. Kubek died. She'd been his landlady for nine years, going back to when Erich and Alison were newlyweds. The duplex in Rogers Park was their first place together. The building backed up against the Metra train tracks, separated by a fence and a weedy slope of no-man's land. Erich and Alison lived upstairs and had their own entrance while Bonnie Kubek lived downstairs with the tiny patch of yard and a fat little dog named Spud. Mrs. Kubek had taken a shine to Alison and on warm Sunday afternoons they drank tea at a little metal table in the yard with her apartment windows open and a Glenn Miller album blasting "In the Mood." When a Metra train roared by, for three seconds the air vibrated and you couldn't hear the music. Spud barked soundlessly, his jaws moving as if in a silent movie. Erich looked down from the upstairs window and Spud looked up and met his eyes and then went to a corner of the yard to shit.

Alison ran errands for Bonnie Kubek and sometimes Erich did, too. A half-gallon of milk, a pound of bananas. Or taking a prescription to the pharmacy. Bonnie entrusted Alison with a key when she went to visit her sister in Waukesha. That was the arrangement, and why wouldn't it last?

But things smashed to hell when Alison took up with her professor at a summer theater camp and a short time later announced that she wanted a divorce. ("Rodney and I are in love. I don't know how it happened, Erich. I'm so sorry.") In what felt like twenty seconds, she moved out. In those days Erich had been drinking a lot and now he was drinking all the time. He could no longer find the off switch. He didn't know where to look, or if he did, he was afraid. The inside of his head became his least favorite place to visit. Bonnie Kubek stopped talking to him after the morning Erich's jeep ended up parked on her front lawn, far beyond the curb, with its front tires in her ferns and the bumper just inches from her living room window. When Erich saw it the next day, looking down from his apartment, he couldn't believe his eyes. But his head throbbed and he had cotton-mouth and he couldn't remember how he got home the previous night, either. Hurriedly he pulled on his pants and pounded down the stairs and started the jeep and backed out of the front yard and parked it correctly in the street. Jogging back to his door, he discovered an ugly dark gash on the lawn where the sod was ripped. Erich knelt and used his hands to comb grass on either side, in an attempt to mask it. Then he ran upstairs. But, gazing down from his upper window, he could still see the scar.

Everything was changing—and nothing could be undone. In the fall, Bonnie's sister in Waukesha died and, not long after, Spud died. Bonnie was very broken up and started speaking to Erich again. She asked him to dig a hole in the back yard to bury the dog. This was illegal in city limits but Bonnie was distraught at the thought of other methods of disposal and wanted to keep Spud nearby. Erich dug the hole, and at dusk he lowered his body, wrapped in a knitted afghan, while she looked on, holding a handkerchief to her mouth.

A few months later, on a warmish day after the New Year—one of those January thaws when all the snow melts and slush floods the gutters and the sun feels deceptively warm and you could almost believe it was Spring and even birds sing in the leafless branches, the fools—Bonnie Kubek walked to Galeazzi's butchers for some spiced sausage and was telling the cashier that she was grateful for the warm day when she could leave the house without fear of slipping on ice and breaking a bone. The cashier looked down to her drawer to make change, and then looked up in time to see Mrs. Kubek clutching the counter, gasping, before she slipped to the floor. She was already dead when the ambulance arrived.

That was the story Erich heard. Heart attack. Her funeral was on a Wednesday and Erich had a convention show that afternoon in Arlington Heights, so he was unable to attend. Mrs. Kubek had been a regular churchgoer and Erich supposed that the other old ladies at St. Joseph's would see to it that she got a proper send-off.

He wondered, though, about his own situation. Who would inherit Bonnie's property? Would they raise his rent? Would they kick him out? In all those years, even after his parking incident, Mrs. Kubek had never raised his rent. The duplex, like other houses on the block, was getting run down. It needed new siding and the sidewalk was breaking up in places, making it hard for Erich to shovel in winter. Other seasons, dandelions grew between the cracks. In her advanced years, Bonnie hadn't cared to invest in upkeep. She was accustomed to her little place and her pokey habits and she didn't want or need anything different. Erich had never heard Bonnie speak of heirs.

In the meantime, Erich collected her mail. After sorting out the junk, he let himself in her apartment with the key Bonnie had originally shared with Alison and he put the mail on the kitchen table. He closed the curtains, because he didn't want anybody peeking in the windows or feeling tempted to break into an unoccupied unit. Burglaries in the neighborhood were on the rise.

A month went by, and Erich didn't pay his rent. How could he? To whom? Even if he'd wanted to, he wouldn't have known how. Besides, it was a welcome respite at a time when his credit card balance was bad and his jeep needed repairs.

The next month was the same. And the month after. He wondered when Mrs. Kubek's people were going to get their act together.

In April, when a pair of gangly daffodils insisted on blooming by Bonnie's back fence, not far from where Spud was buried, events took a more decisive turn. Erich came home and checked the mailbox and found an envelope with a conspicuous red band and the words FINAL NOTICE printed on the outside. He knew what this meant. The utility bills. By now the kitchen table downstairs was piled high with envelopes, but for the first time he took the liberty of opening Bonnie's mail. He set his mouth grimly and ripped the top flap.

Yes: it was an ultimatum. If she didn't pay the balance, the electricity and water would be cut off, effective in fifteen days.

So what to do? Their duplex still had an old system of shared meters. The arrangement had always been that Mrs. Kubek showed Alison—or later, Erich—the electric and water bills, and she accepted payment in cash. The meters were in her name. It was actually another perk of the upstairs unit since the old lady didn't take many showers and much of her heating rose to the next level. This kept costs down.

This time, Erich didn't hesitate. He wrote out a check to pay the utilities and dropped it in the mail. He kept the stub, intending to claim this sum from the heirs, whenever they materialized. At the time of this transaction, it should also be said, Erich was attending A.A. and hadn't had a drink for months. His sponsor Fred Cunningham always shook his hand and said when they parted, "Remember, kid. I got your back." Old Fred had a bald lumpy head, bad teeth and a doglike face; he'd been sober for over ten years and lived by himself in a little shitbox efficiency on Auburn Avenue. He always wore the same brown pants that didn't fit. But he seemed so grateful to be alive, laughing heartily whenever Erich attempted a small joke, that his optimism was strangely contagious. Fred meant his words, and nothing bad that Erich might say or do was going to impress him. *"I got your back."* He was happy, he was loyal, and you couldn't bullshit him. Despite appearances, you wanted to be like Fred. That was the mystery of his Fredness. So Erich decided not to worry that he was paying no rent. He would trust his good fortune, and be glad.

By August he'd caught up on his debts and his credit card was in a sweet black spot it hadn't known in years. He was still sober and he'd started lifting weights again, an activity he'd enjoyed as a teenager, and he liked what he saw in the mirror. He performed close-up three nights a week at the Althea Dinner Theater out in Northwood, going from table to table, and his routines were well-received, eliciting a very positive buzz. Tips were good. He also worked mornings at Wendall's, an urban truck farm in Lincolnwood which grew hydroponic microgreens beneath LED lights. He helped with rotating and cleaning trays, and he drove an emerald WOO van (*Wendall's Original Organics*, said large lettering on the side) to deliver the goods to food subscribers around the city. From one day to the next, Erich was busy.

Downstairs at the duplex, Bonnie Kubek's kitchen table was overflowing with mail. A pair of her brown shoes still waited on a neat square of newspaper by the back door; her winter scarves hung from a hook; a clock ticked above the refrigerator. This atmosphere, as if Bonnie had just stepped out on an errand and might return any minute, had felt spooky at first, but now Erich was used to it. He'd started a second stack of mail on a kitchen chair, all the while keeping a sharp eye out for anything that required his attention.

One day a yellow window envelope landed in Bonnie's box, from the Cook County tax office. Erich tore it open and discovered it was actually a reminder that she'd missed a previous installment. He frowned and looked at the heaps of mail. Probably it was in there, somewhere—it must've sneaked by him. Now the second installment was due.

The situation was awkward, but also obvious. As far as officialdom was concerned, Bonnie Kubek was still alive. As long as she kept paying, that was her claim to existence.

The tax was $1849.17. A big chunk, sure. . .but if he kept things square with the gods in power, why, this could go on for years!

Thus began a new phase in Erich's relationship with Mrs. Kubek. He paid all the bills in her name promptly, and he cut her tiny patch of grass.

The following spring he weeded around the crazy-ass daffodils, which had sprung up again. "Hey Spud," he said out of the corner of his mouth, looking at the burial spot. "You weren't a bad dog."

Witnesses

HE'D ALWAYS ASSUMED that a long-lost nephew or distant cousin would one day knock on his door, and that would be the end of it. Of course the penny would drop, one of these days. Months? Years? Maybe a Chicago city employee or functionary flunky of Cook County would catch him in some overlooked paperwork. The snare of bureaucracy. But no. What got him were the real estate developers, those connivers.

"Do you rent this apartment?"

A shiny-faced kid with an electronic tablet, standing at his door on a Saturday morning. She consulted her screen. "Records say this place belongs to Ms. Agnes B. Kubek but she doesn't answer her mail and her land line has been disconnected. Can you help me?"

Erich hadn't seen the point of paying for a phone. (Really, was that anybody's business?) On this occasion, he volunteered no information, feigning ignorance. The next three times that real estate representatives appeared at his door, he gave them the brush-off. He wasn't particularly concerned. They seemed like low-level busybodies.

But then the tone changed. Unmistakably, people became more inquisitive, even suspicious. "Why is she never home? When did you last see her?"

"Oh, I spoke to her just last week," said Erich. "We talked about the Cubs. She hasn't got back to you?" Erich mused for a moment. "Maybe she's visiting her sister in Houston. Or was it Fort Worth? I don't remember. If you can, check out Texas."

He shut the door.

To another inquisitor he said, "Mrs. Kubek wants to be left alone. She doesn't like to answer her door to strangers. Security, you know, these days. . ."

By then Erich had started sneaking in her back door to turn on her lights for a part of the evening, just to keep up appearances. Luckily the previous neighbors across the fence had moved out and had been replaced by an Indian family who knew nothing of Bonnie or of what had happened one January thaw.

"*Buy* this property?"

Erich repeated these words back to a new petitioner at his doorstep. He hadn't seen this guy before, a thin fellow in a gray suit whose tenacious manner made it clear that he wanted to come inside. If that happened, Erich knew, he was asking for trouble. The guy was like a sinister combination of an evangelist and a junkie in need of a fix. Erich blocked the threshold.

"I'll tell you, just between ourselves." Erich rubbed his chin. "Mrs. Kubek doesn't want to sell. She's mentioned it to me on a number of occasions. She's lived here since World War II and is very attached to this place. She gets angry if you bring up the subject. I wouldn't go there, if I were you."

He shut the door.

Like mushrooms, FOR SALE signs popped up on lawns of his block. When demolition of two buildings across the street began, he knew something larger was afoot. Even so, the summons from the FBI astonished him. This was his first meeting with Agent Heffernan.

"Why on earth would you pay your landlord's property tax?" she asked.

"Why is that a problem?" Erich answered. He knew better than to say anything inexact with a person of her capacity. "Since when do people in this country get in trouble for paying taxes?"

"Well, she's dead. As I'm sure you know."

Erich didn't reply. It wasn't really a question, so he didn't need to say anything. That part of Bonnie's situation wasn't his fault. But it was hard to sit still. He hated it when people condescended to him. It had happened just minutes ago, at the beginning of the interview, when she'd asked him about his occupation, and Erich had replied that he was a magician. Her reaction was depressingly typical. If he'd introduced himself as an actor, she might've said, "Oh really? That's interesting. What have you been in?" Or if he'd asserted he was a musician: "What do you play?" But the word *magician* triggered a different response in people, as if they expected a guy in a cheesy tuxedo, or maybe a brown-toothed carny. They had a narrow conception of winners and losers, a lack of imagination about the pursuit of excellence. Agent Heffernan smiled (a *tolerant* smile) and told him, "I used to do magic tricks when I was a kid." Erich was tempted to reply, "Yeah, well, I used to play cops and robbers." But he remained silent. He nodded blandly, because he couldn't afford to get on her bad side.

Now she said, "Your handling of form 7551 in Mrs. Kubek's name constitutes identify theft. And there are other legal issues involved if, as it appears, you are an undeclared beneficiary."

Oh God, Erich thought. *Make it stop.*

"Have you heard of Westbrook Developments?" she asked.

Erich nodded. That was the name on the signs on lawns in his neighborhood. He'd also seen it on billboards around the city, and on the business cards that busybodies had left in Bonnie's mail slot.

"Westbrook is buying up property. They've already got most of the units on your block. They want to put in high-rises and a new shopping complex."

This news didn't please Erich but he wasn't surprised. Neighborhoods were always changing. Still, it was better to keep the conversation about those people rather than about him. "How's that against the law?"

"It's not. But somebody has to pay for it."

Why was she looking at him that way?

The *Ahhts*

ERICH TOLD HIS FRIEND Tom Denison about his interviews with Agent Heffernan. He could trust Tom. He and Tom went way back. In middle school, they'd performed in talent contests together; they'd sat next to each other on the bench for the sophomore football team at St. Jerome's. Years later, Tom was at the after-show party where Erich had first met Alison Keating. If there had been a public wedding ceremony (Erich and Alison had eloped), Tom would've been the best man. Instead, Tom got the job of helping Erich carry furniture upstairs one hot weekend when the newlyweds moved into Bonnie Kubek's duplex.

Unlike Erich, Tom had stuck it out in college and had earned a degree from Northwestern. From the "Department of The*atre*," as the place insisted on calling itself. Sometimes Tom put on a plummy accent and joked, "I gave my life to the *ahhts*." He'd played Puck and Estragon and Biff Loman, and had shown his musical chops in *Grease*. For years he'd done summer Shakespeare in Wisconsin or upstate New York. More recently he'd taken an office job in the Loop for a video streaming start up. He was still paying back his student loans. After years of sharing cramped apartments with theater people and once, a sprawling old house with a political activist commune called "Tomorrow, Tomorrow, and Tomorrow" (what a dump that place was!), Tom had moved back in with his parents. It was a major change. Still, Erich detected no disappointment on Tom's part, or a sense of abandoned dreams. The last time they'd spoken, Tom had sounded relieved. Now he spent his days in a bright clean office before going home to Mom's meatloaf. Recently he'd turned down a chorus role in *The Pirates of Penzance*.

Erich met him at a coffee shop called Premiums near Tom's office building. It was disorienting to see his friend in a tailored shirt and tie, with his company's photo ID hanging from a lanyard, and impossible to shake the impression that Tom was in costume for another part, albeit a better-playing one than his previous gigs. He could've been on his way to the makeup chair. Tom announced that he didn't have much time, so Erich plunged right in, telling him what he'd done after Bonnie's death.

"So this cop lady or agent or whatever the hell she really is, she's talking like maybe charges won't be pressed against me, if I do them a favor. But she's coy about what the favor would be. It's like I'm supposed to accept before I know what it is. And how do I know she can deliver on her end? She's no prosecutor or judge. Maybe I'll just get jerked around."

"Westbrook is all that Russian gas money, you know," said Tom.

"Yeah, I know, but that has nothing to do with me."

In truth, Erich had known this fact for only a few hours, after doing some hasty Internet searches in an attempt to fill in the gaps after his interview with Agent Heffernan. He'd found the name in local business reporting.

"Probably money-laundering," Tom said. "These guys got all this cash and it's a headache about where to put it, what to do with it next. Real estate is legitimate. Property is respectable. If they're going to develop a neighborhood and pay a bunch of local taxes, the city isn't going to ask too many questions about where the money came from. Hell, I bet aldermen have already rolled out the red carpet. What's the guy's name again?"

"Plutov," said Erich.

"Yeah, that's the one. I've heard of him. He married an American, I think."

"So what should I do?"

"What *can* you do?" Tom asked. "You don't want to cross the FBI. It's better to keep people like that on your side."

Erich knew that Tom was right and the rest of their conversation circled around this fact, though there was nothing satisfying about it. Erich repeated what he'd read about Plutov, that upon his arrival in the United States he'd worked in the dry-cleaning business. He'd started in West Town and a few other locations before he got big.

"And now he's buying up your block?" Tom laughed. "That's a hell of a lot of dry-cleaning." He stood and replaced the plastic lid on his coffee cup. "I got to go, man. Can I have your lid? We got a deal with Premiums at my company. There's a special card and we get an environmental discount."

Erich gave him his cup lid.

"See you at the top!" Tom said.

It was a parting expression they'd used for years, a joke about future success.

"Yeah," Erich said. "Anything for the *ahhts*."

Enter Mr. Boots

AFTER THEIR CAKE AND ICE-CREAM, the kids were hyped, jacked up on sugar, screaming and bouncing into each other. Erich wheeled out his table and waited for them to settle. Suddenly, heads turned.

"It's Batman!"

Serena swept through the throng of children, her cape billowing above their heads. They shouted in delight.

"To the rescue!"

Her performance was simple but effective, a cameo from a recognizable star. They hooted and cheered and Serena played along, striking poses, buoyed by their boisterousness. When the cries eventually subsided, she invited them to chat with her, answering the kids' questions in a deep, gravelly voice that Erich couldn't help finding sexy. Images of their encounter upstairs flickered in his mind. She let the children touch her black leather gloves. Viktor pressed forward and talked more avidly than the others. He seemed pleased with his masked Momma.

Erich waited his turn to perform, occasionally sneaking a peek at the back of his table to make sure that Boots the rabbit was comfortable and getting plenty of air. Boots was concealed in a recessed shelf of black wire mesh, where he placidly munched on alfalfa pellets that Erich had poured along the edge. He seemed unperturbed by the noise. No stage-fright for Boots.

Erich had rented the rabbit and other kid-show equipment including the Shanghai Mystery Box from an acquaintance named Greg Griffin, a man with a Mephistophelean goatee and dramatic moustache to which he applied liberal amounts of wax. Greg had a day job at a Mitsubishi dealership but he fancied himself an entertainer. Erich had seen his act at a local magic club, Ring 43 of the International Brotherhood of Magicians, which met monthly at a nearby steakhouse and provided an opportunity for hobbyists to try out their tricks. Greg's show was a mess of clichéd stunts, stilted patter and bad timing. The guy was dreadful. But that didn't stop him from advertising in the Yellow Pages and on his website as *"Grinnin' Griffin, Chicago's Finest Conjuror."* He was surely one of Chicago's cheapest conjurors, undercutting the rates of seasoned performers and giving parents all over the city second thoughts about ever again hiring a magician.

"So how'd you get this gig?" Greg had asked him point blank. He knew that Erich didn't ordinarily do children's shows, and he sounded jealous. "Who is it?"

Greg was leading him along his driveway to his back yard, where he'd built a rabbit hutch.

"Somebody I don't know," Erich said. "Can't remember the name off the top of my head. I wrote it down."

Greg threw a suspicious glance over his shoulder and kept walking. They ducked under a clothesline and approached a toolshed, against which stood the hutch. It was a solid structure of planks and chicken-wire. "I got Lucy and Gibber and Boots. They're all good rabbits, first-rate pros. I guess I'd recommend good old Mr. Boots. He's got a strong bladder, if you're going to be out all day."

He reached inside and extracted a waddling white ball of fur, holding it by the scruff of the neck. Boots kicked the air a couple of times and then hung still, as if resigned or too fat and lazy to bother. Erich noticed his hind feet, the color of charcoal.

"Remember," said Greg, "*Never* lift a rabbit by the ears. That can be very painful. Hold him like this."

"I know," said Erich impatiently. He didn't like being patronized by the likes of Grinnin' Griffin. He counted out fifty dollars for renting the rabbit and equipment. In this conversation, Erich suspected that Greg was over-compensating, that he was intimidated. Not by anything Erich said, but by the fact that Erich was a professional, like his parents and grandparents before him. He had a reputation. Erich wasn't a snob about it but for those who bothered to know, the Ambrose family was something of a magic dynasty in the Chicago area. Outsiders always asked, "*Erich?* That's how you spell your name? 'Eric' with an 'h'?" He nodded patiently. Yes, that was right.

Insiders, though, never asked. "Erich" was obviously a tribute to Erich Weiss, the immigrant child from Budapest who became famous in America as Harry Houdini. Back when he was still Weiss (or Erik Weisz, or Ehrich. . .he was a changeable man), he'd befriended a juggler named Ollie Ambrose. They'd worked together in a dime museum on Wabash Avenue, where Ollie spun plates and Weiss performed card manipulations for ten hours a day, alongside contortionists, shadow artists and limbless individuals displaying their congenital infirmities. Ollie and Weiss became bosom pals, and late in life Houdini wrote to him with thanks for his inspiration in show business. (Erich now owned this letter, and kept it in a safety deposit box.) In magic circles, this history was pure gold. It was like knowing Louis Armstrong before he was, well, *Louis Armstrong.*

"I must leave you now," Batman told the circle of children. "New challenges await me!" She teetered slightly, unsteady on her feet, and then rushed out of the room. Erich wondered if she was going to be sick.

Her sudden absence was palpable—as if oxygen had been sucked away—and then, one by one, heads turned around and discovered Erich, standing by his table.

"Yes, it's me—the Amazing Ambrose!"

No one moved. But the dark-haired nanny stepped in and urged the children to return to their chairs. It took a couple of minutes before they settled in.

Erich began his show with a rope routine, followed by "tricky science," which was basically a running gag with his "magnetic wand." It made the kids laugh, though. They followed his cues, playing along.

All the while, doubts loomed in the back of his mind about the upcoming Shanghai Mystery Box. He studied the children's faces, searching for likely volunteers, anticipating how to push this stunt past them. The trick might be too old-fashioned and corny for this group. Immature they were, sure, but they also possessed a sophistication that was a 21st century kind of ignorance, insulating them from old-fashioned wonder. A magical *rabbit*? Would they care? But he'd taken the trouble to rent and transport the equipment and the critter for this show, so he pressed on.

"Who likes to draw?" Erich asked. "I bet you love to draw. You can let your imagination run free!"

A few children nodded, some looked at him stony-faced while others, he suspected, hadn't even registered his question. They fidgeted and avoided eye contact. An unpleasant reminiscence flashed upon him of an early A.A. meeting, before he met Fred Cunningham, a dark period in his life. ("*Who wants to share?*") But this was supposed to be fun! Erich put on a big smile.

"Viktor!" he exclaimed. "I'm sure you're an artist."

Viktor shrugged. As the honored birthday boy, he seemed a logical choice. And he didn't appear to be the type to wilt under attention. The trick could be directed to him.

Erich held out a pad and a sharpie. Viktor accepted them and waited. "Okay, everybody!" Erich said. "If Viktor were a magician, what kind of animal do you think he'd do a trick with?"

"An elephant!"

"An eagle!"

"An orca!"

It took a surprisingly long time to elicit a *rabbit* from their young imaginations, but eventually Erich got them to say it and he persuaded Viktor to draw a bunny, along with an elephant and a bird, in order to provide the illusion of choice. Then he mixed up the sketches and allowed a member of the audience to "choose" one at random. With an underflip, Erich forced the rabbit on the audience.

"Now which one did you pick? Oh, look—a rabbit! *Thank you.* Viktor sure did a wonderful drawing. Let's give him a round of applause."

The kids clapped.

"And here," Erich said, pointing to his table, "We have the Shanghai Mystery Box, where the powers of the imagination enter. . .reality!"

The box was a black-lacquered rectangle with a red Chinese character on the side. The appearance made Erich wince. This was the sort of equipment that had already looked hokey to Erich when he was a child. He couldn't imagine how it would appear to this group, nurtured on Play Stations and touchscreens. Powers of the imagination? It was like inviting these kids to play a game of "telephone" with a pair of tin cans and a string.

"As you can see, it is perfectly empty." He lifted the rectangle and tilted it in the air. This was the only part of the trick where a bit of technique was necessary, as well as timing, because he had to set the box down very neatly on its marks in order to slide Boots soundlessly from his loading chamber behind the table. If the corners weren't positioned correctly, the box could jam. Over the years, Erich had witnessed a number of bad performers who, at the very moment a light touch was required, suddenly stiffened and grimaced and handled the "empty" container like a hod of bricks.

"But if I insert your wonderful drawing into the Shanghai Mystery Box, where philosophers from the Far East volunteered their cogitations, we enter another dimension."

Erich was positive that the kids hadn't a goddamn clue of what he was talking about. But there was no stopping now! And, however much he disliked this trick in someone else's hands, he took a masochistic pleasure in doing it himself, in respecting the outdated form. This was a piece of parlor magic from the Victorian era, a heritage of show business culture, in its way a valid element of the ramshackle civilization of which these spoiled children were unaware. This was part of history, and he would inflict it on them. Eat your spinach!

"Your drawing will be actualized to its fullest potential," he announced.

Erich slid the paper into the lid. He smiled as he lightly levered the load shelf and slotted Boots into the box, avoiding jerky movements. He lifted the "empty" rectangle, feigning that it was very light, though his wrists felt considerable strain. Good Lord, he thought. Boots is a fat boy.

He approached the children. "And what do we have?"

He reached inside, grabbed Boots by the scruff. He lifted him, kicking, in the air.

"Your rabbit!"

Sure, the trick was crude, it was obvious, it was as subtle as the *whoomp* of a slide trombone. But no doubt about it, the appearance of a live rabbit made an impression. It was a good payoff even for this crowd. "Ohhhh!" they said. "Hey!" The Shanghai Mystery Box was manifestly fake, but big fat Boots was indisputably real, a soft furry squirming PRESENCE. You couldn't get *this* on a smart phone. A bulging bunny. *Alive.*

Erich brought him closer so that they could touch him. "Easy now, just a nice stroke there." He brought him to Viktor. "This is the work of your imagination."

Viktor reached out.

Later, thinking back on this moment, Erich could remember nothing amiss. Viktor made no sudden gesture. It wasn't the kid's fault. Although he'd acted like a brat earlier, there was nothing objectionable in his behavior now, nothing different from the other kids. But for some reason, when Viktor reached out, Boots panicked. His whole body juddered and he jerked his head forward and bit.

"Ow!"

It happened swiftly but it wasn't over swiftly; for two long seconds, Boots seemed to hang on to Viktor's thumb; there was enough time for Viktor to stamp his feet in place before Boots let go.

"Ow! Ow! Ow!"

Now Viktor stumbled back, clutching his thumb in front of him. It bubbled red.

"Ayeee!"

Erich was temporarily speechless, gripping Boots by the scruff. But then, as Viktor danced away, and for reasons he couldn't explain, he let out a nervous laugh. It jumped out of him. This wasn't derision; Erich was no sadist. He was very surprised, shocked even, and no doubt reacting in panic. In all his years of witnessing and performing magic shows, he'd never seen anything like it.

"It's not funny!" Viktor shouted. He pressed his thumb against his chest, staining his shirt.

Now the nanny surged forward. "Let me see that, Viktor. Oh my. Come on, let's go to the sink."

The following minutes went by in a blur. Erich stuffed Boots back into his box and followed them into the kitchen, leaving the stunned children to their own devices. "Sorry!" he exclaimed. "It was an accident. You know, extremities can bleed a lot but it's probably not as bad as it looks."

"Please go," the nanny said. "We don't have time to talk now." She held out a washcloth. "Viktor, I'm going to apply some pressure with this. Okay? It won't hurt more, I promise." She shot a glance at Erich. "Go!"

So Erich hastily gathered up his affairs, closed his table and wheeled his way out. As he left the dining area to exit through the kitchen, he caught a glimpse of Serena coming down the staircase, dressed as a pirate, wearing flowing linen pants and a broad leather belt and an eye-patch. He kept going.

Surprises and Secrets

ELL, YOU COULDN'T plan everything. Whose fault was that? There were always surprises. Improvisation was a fact of life. As a teenager he'd set up a table and performed on Sunday mornings before football games outside the Roosevelt Road El as Bears fans streamed toward Soldier Field. There were saxophone players, break-dancers, all kinds of buskers, competing for the attention of thousands of excited people. The air rippled with anticipation. In those days Erich lacked experience and his technique was uneven but already he'd found his close up vocation and his favorite routine: the mug and egg. It was a stripped-down version of the classic shell game or cups and balls, using only a ceramic coffee mug like you found in diners, and a hard-boiled egg. The egg disappeared and reappeared; Erich put the egg in his jacket pocket, yet somehow the egg always came back under the mug. Next, Erich would pause, tap the egg against his forehead to crack the shell and then began to peel it, telling a joke and inviting his spectators to throw money in the jar in front of his table. Suddenly, a salt shaker appeared under the mug, which he used to sprinkle a few grains on his peeled egg before taking a bite. "Come on!" he coaxed the crowd, pointing to the tip jar. "Help a man eat!" If a heckler got in the way, and persisted, Erich included the intruder in his act, inviting him hold an egg while a second or a third egg appeared, keeping the heckler busy, till the moment came to have a snack, and Erich tapped the egg on his forehead. He began to peel the egg. "Come on, join me," he said, and when the heckler followed his example, the egg crushed against his forehead. It was raw, of course. "Wow!" Erich said. "How did you do that?"

Surprises were part of the job. Secrets, however, were of a different order—another kind of performance.

When Erich was a child, his parents had teamed up for a stage act called "A Touch of Ambrosia" and, back in the day, it was very slick, even fashionable. Their show featured a climatic sequence of his father in a glittering jacket dancing to disco music around his mother, magically producing doves from silk kerchiefs. She stood beaming, rocking her hips, the décolleté of her dress revealing considerable cleavage. Her bare, dimpled arms stretched outward, and the magic unfurled: one-two-three-four-five-six doves perched on her wings! Erich's mother looked as if she might fly away, a voluptuous scarecrow.

"This was when dove acts were all the rage," Erich explained to Alison. He'd pulled an old VHS tape out of a box and plugged it in. "A dove will compact small and it's easy to conceal, and when you pull it out, it gets excited and flutters, so it suddenly looks big, which is a dramatic effect."

Alison was laughing. "This is a hoot!" She wasn't paying attention to Erich's description of the magic. "Look at his white boy afro! And your mom's dress! Wow!"

"Yeah," said Erich. Maybe he shouldn't have shown her this tape. It was embarrassing. Even as a child, this sequence had made him uncomfortable. All that wiggling.

"You can tell your dad is gay. It's obvious, isn't it?"

"You think so?"

His question was disingenuous. Sure, watching the tape now, it was easy to come to that conclusion. But that wasn't the whole story. When he was a kid, it had seemed anything but obvious. It wasn't only a question of styles, which were perceived differently in those days. Fact was, the subject had never come up, not in Erich's presence. Not once! All he remembered was that when his parents split up, he'd moved in with his granddad Lou. The immediate source of crisis and upheaval was that his mother Luanne had gone on a bender with a frozen foods salesman from Wausau, Wisconsin. That much he knew. When this happened, his father Danny suddenly moved to California. That much was said aloud, too. Apparently his father was staying with a friend named Jerry, but nothing was explained about Jerry and it hadn't occurred to Erich to inquire about their relationship. He was a trusting child, and his granddad Lou was kind to him, gentle and solicitous. And all the while, though the situation was upsetting, the turmoil didn't *shock* Erich. Many of his school friends also had divorcing parents and they shifted from house to house. In a dismaying way, he discovered himself to be typical. This was an additional source of unhappiness. He'd been brought up to believe that the Ambroses were extraordinary.

Granddad Lou tended bar at Schaefer's, an old-fashioned tavern on the north side, famous for its dark beer and corned-beef sandwiches. Lou did close-up tricks for customers and enjoyed a considerable reputation both in and out of magic circles. He told salty stories of celebrities and politicians he'd fooled at the bar, including Hollywood people and sports stars. Mike

Royko had mentioned him in his columns in the *Sun-Times,* and there was a period when he was on a first-name basis with Leo Durocher and Dick Butkus. His specialty was sleight-of-hand with cigarettes, which appeared and disappeared in his fingers with amusing rapidity. His broken and restored cigarette routine was truly masterful, his signature piece, which he'd developed back in the 1950s and thereafter executed with idiosyncratic perfection, like an early rock and roll classic. This routine had a lasting influence and ripple effect and it was imitated by subsequent generations of performers but no one, Erich knew with pride, could do it with the same offbeat charm and timing as Lou. (More than a decade after Lou's death, he'd watched a YouTube video of some guy with earrings in São Paulo performing a broken-and-restored sequence that was obviously indebted to Lou's handling: it was technically accomplished but lacked nuance, such as the way Lou's chin had leaned in, creating another plane of surfaces, or the deadpan theater of how Lou himself appeared surprised, even helpless, before the miracle happening at his fingertips.) Granddad Lou had schooled Erich on cigarettes, cards and coins, and was directly responsible for his love of challenging sleight of hand. From the age of fifteen Erich had spent a lot of time at the bar—laws were less strictly enforced in that neighborhood—and though only a blue-jeaned skinny kid with a cowlick which refused to slick down, in Schaefer's Tavern Erich found a second home. He hung out with his granddad's cronies and heard all the old stories. When Lou saw that he was sincerely interested in the art, he took Erich under his wing and shared his techniques, the accumulation of decades of experience. His grandfather was a generous teacher, unlike many performers, and he learned all the old man's moves.

Most importantly, he taught Erich basic principles that went beyond particular sleights or tricks. These precepts would mark his attitudes toward life. Lou pointed out how the world was full of hacks doing the same old routines, what he referred to as the *same old shit*. In the presence such acts, his grandfather muttered under his breath, "S.O.S." His way of saying, "Get me outta here!" For Lou, it was fundamental that a performance should violate what was familiar. It should take you Somewhere Else. ("This is magic, ain't it?") Lou also stressed that much of the difficulty lay, paradoxically, in keeping it simple. Some conjurors tried to avoid the *same old shit* by introducing complications, fussing and performing pirouettes, but for Lou that was *getting lost in your own noodles*. Watching these acts was like experiencing a frustrating dream that didn't deliver: you tossed and turned and desired it to come together, but it unreeled and tangled and left you unsatisfied. Lou's exquisite handling of the broken and restored cigarette was of a different order, largely because of its simplicity. Look: what was lost, irreparably damaged and seemingly irretrievable—it came back! Was *whole* again. Wasn't that a possibility, a Somewhere Else, you wanted to exist? A humble, everyday evocation of Eden—or was it like rolling away the stone of Lazarus' tomb? It repaired the inexorable consequences of Time. It was a waking dream that matched the yearning of your heart.

Erich's father, Danny Ambrose, died in a boating accident near Weebanks, California, shortly before his son graduated from high school. Erich didn't attend the funeral. No one in the family made the trip. Barely a year later, granddad Lou died of melanoma. The diagnosis came out of the blue. Bourbon and cigarettes hadn't killed Lou, but the sun, which he'd avoided all his working life, proved his undoing. Lou went down fast. Erich grieved as if it had been his father. At the age of eighteen, so much was broken and could not be restored. There was only a gaping absence. With a certainty he didn't possess about other subjects, such as how to make a living or what to think about politics or any of those time-consuming questions that seemed to preoccupy other people, Erich knew that his future would be devoted to addressing what was already gone. He felt angry, badly tricked.

A few years later, when Erich and Alison were living upstairs in Bonnie Kubek's duplex, the phone rang late one night.

"Hello. Is this Erich Ambrose?"

"Yes. Who is this?"

"I'm Jerry Teasdale. I was close to your dad. Could I have a few minutes of your time?"

"Uh. . . Okay. I guess so."

Maybe Erich should've expected this call, but he wasn't ready for it. He listened numbly while Jerry told him what a great guy Danny was, how frequently he'd spoken of his son and how he'd been intending to get in touch with Erich before the accident. "It was all so sudden—just unbelievable. He missed you," Jerry said. "He had high hopes for you. Why didn't you come to the funeral?"

This question made Erich angry. Was that any of his business? "I don't have to justify myself to you. You call me at midnight to ask me *that*? For fuck's sake!"

The truth was, he'd wanted very much to attend the funeral but in the end, he'd ceded to his mother's wishes. She'd urged him to come visit her in Florida, insisted that his true family was down there, not out in California. So he went to Pensacola. Luanne Ambrose had sobered up and remarried and started a new life with a preacher named Brice. "That fellow, that Jerry Teasdale, he was *bad news*," she'd told him on this visit. This was the first time Erich had heard her speak of Jerry, but apparently she'd been acquainted with him before she and Danny had split up. "He was one of those skinny slinky boys that used to hang out at the Happy Cat Club. Your dad and I worked there sometimes. Jerry wore the tightest pants I've ever seen. Frankly, I don't know how he managed to walk. To this day I struggle not to hate him. I work on that. 'Hate the sin, not the sinner.'"

"*Oh please please please,*" Jerry Teasdale implored years later on the telephone. "Don't be angry, Erich. Your father loved you, you know that, right? I owe it to him to remind you. God, I. . .I just miss him so much!"

And now Jerry was blubbering at the other end of the line. Erich felt very uncomfortable. He didn't have anything to say to this man. He wished he'd cut the conversation short, before it got sloppy. There were too many unwelcome questions.

But then something shifted inside him. Maybe it was the tone of Jerry's voice, more than his words. The man was obviously sincere. Still grieving. Was it possible to share a pain with someone you'd never met?

Suddenly, Erich was crying, too. Recalling his father. "He said he was going to come see me," he choked out. "He told me that more than once."

"I know. But Lou begged him to hold off. He didn't think you were ready."

"What do you mean? Of course I was ready."

"Lou thought otherwise, Erich. He didn't like me."

"But we're not talking about you! It's *me!* Me and my dad."

"I know. That's what he said, too."

Erich heard himself breathing hard. For a long time it was the only sound.

"I hope you don't blame him," Jerry added.

The conversation lasted almost an hour. Not all of it was deeply personal or revisiting the past. Erich learned that Jerry sold water softener salts for a living. Jerry was delighted to learn that Erich had continued the family tradition of magic. "Oh that's *cool*, fella," he said. "And you're married! Congratulations!" But inevitably the conversation circled back to the subject of Danny Ambrose.

"Listen, I didn't mean to upset you," Jerry told him. "But I needed to share. Sometimes things are too much to hold in. Say—is it okay if I call again sometime?"

"Well. . .all right." Erich had nothing more to say to the man, but he figured: what difference would it make?

And Jerry Teasdale did call occasionally, often very late. Times zones didn't interest him. He also developed a weird chatty relationship with Alison. Sometimes she picked up the phone first and they gabbed as if they were old pals, talking about the weather in California or about a play she was auditioning for. Erich couldn't fathom this—what was the point? She had no connection with Jerry. Even more inexplicable was the stab of jealousy Erich experienced as he waited for her to hand him the phone.

A few months after Alison left him and started shacking up with Professor Barnes ("fucking Rodney Barnes," was how Erich mentally referred to him), Jerry and Erich became friends on a social media website. Jerry posted pictures of himself and corgi dogs going down a water slide into a swimming pool. Jerry was ruddy and plump, and wore enormous sunglasses; his skinny, slinky days were definitely behind him.

When Erich mentioned his new relationship with Jerry to his mother, she was not pleased, which was no surprise, but her attitude toward the man seemed to have mellowed. "Oh, for goodness sake, *that guy?* What a drip." She laughed hoarsely. "You know, he's not the one that really bugs me. The person I'm mad at is Lou."

"Granddad? Why?"

"Well, he knew. He knew all along."

"What? What did he know?"

"About your dad. He never breathed a word to me in all those years, both before and after we were married. Jerry wasn't the first one for your dad, understand what I'm saying? If I'd known it earlier, I wouldn't have married him."

"But—"

Erich didn't finish his sentence, and his mother kept talking, recounting a wedding anecdote that he'd already heard before, about her allergic reaction to a floral arrangement. He didn't listen. *But what about me?* Erich wanted to ask. *If you hadn't married him, I wouldn't exist.*

Still, she didn't mean any harm, not really. And it dawned on him that he shared her anger with Lou.

His grandfather had been ashamed of his son. He'd never spoken to Erich—not once!—about Jerry Teasdale and a basic aspect of Danny Ambrose's life. He'd taught Erich to perform so many surprises, all the while keeping this secret, denying him, playing up to a lie. Sure, Lou was a man of his generation, full of the old prejudices, but that excuse, Erich thought, wasn't good enough: no, it was the *same old shit*. A failure of imagination. And though Erich could see that much, he couldn't put all the blame on Lou, either. His imagination had often fallen short, too. Struggling to find a way, hadn't he introduced new complications?

Was he lost in his own noodles?

Cherries and Sprinkles

FTER VIKTOR'S BIRTHDAY PARTY, driving his jeep from the leafy streets of Wilmette, Erich tried to cheer himself up. Okay—the show was bad. A flop. Without question, his worst ever. He'd made a terrible exit. His professional pride was bruised.

Still, Mr. Boots' behavior wasn't his fault. Plus, his *real* performance that day wasn't with silly balloon animals or the Shanghai Mystery Box or a nasty rabbit. He'd been on assignment for the FBI, and he'd executed his task superbly, hadn't he? He'd placed monitors all over the house, even in Plutov's bedroom, for God's sake! Agent Heffernan couldn't ask for more than that.

She was expecting him in her office, but before reporting downtown, he exited for Clark Street and swung by Greg Griffin's house to return Boots. Greg had said that he'd be at home. Erich wanted to unload this equipment and the rabbit and wash his hands of the whole affair.

When he rang the doorbell, Greg answered immediately, as if he'd been lingering in the vestibule, anticipating his return. "Hey, Erich."

"Hey." Erich wheeled the table and cage across the threshold.

"Everything go all right?" Greg knelt to the cage and unhooked the strap. "Hey, Mr. Boots! Did you knock their socks off? You da rabbit!"

"Everything was fine," said Erich. "Thanks."

"He's a sexy boy, ain't he?"

"Uh huh."

Greg pulled him out of the cage; Boots' hind legs kicked the air. "Dude! Dude!" He lifted him to eye level. "What's this on his chin?"

Erich was already backing toward the door. "What?"

"His chin, look at it. Have you been feeding him cherries? Man, you can't do that! I know he likes them, but they give him colic. You might think you're being nice but it's not good for him."

"I haven't been feeding him cherries."

Erich observed a streaky patch of red under Boots' lower jaw. He hadn't noticed it earlier. Boots blinked, and Erich experienced a peculiar sensation that Boots understood this conversation and was watching him. "*What happened?*" Greg exclaimed. It was unclear whether he was speaking to Erich or to the rabbit. "Look at those whiskers!"

Boots' nose wrinkled and his mouth twitched. It was like a grimace, or maybe a sour grin.

"He's stressed," said Greg. "Poor fella."

"Listen, I gotta go."

"You sure there's not something you're not telling me?"

"I'm sure."

It was a twenty minute drive to FBI headquarters and when he arrived, he was told to wait in the fourth floor reception area. There was a coffee urn and donuts. Erich filled a big Styrofoam cup and helped himself to a donut with sprinkles. He had time for only one bite before he was summoned.

"How did it go?" she asked, before he even sat down.

"It's all done." Sprinkles were dry in his throat, so he took a big sip of coffee, burning his mouth. It was bad coffee. "I plastered that house with monitors. Upstairs and down. Now you'll hear everything you want."

Agent Heffernan placed her glasses on her nose. They hung from a chain around her neck, and she was always moving them up and down. "We'll see about that. Tell me, did you observe the Plutovs? I mean besides the son. Did you see Andre Plutov?"

"No. He wasn't there."

"Not at his son's birthday party? Really?"

She scribbled on her pad.

"It was just the kids at the magic show. And a nanny." In his mind he heard her saying, "*Go!*" Should he tell Agent Heffernan about that part? He doubted she'd appreciate the practical difficulties of performance.

"His wife? What about her?"

"I saw her, yes."

She scribbled some more. Should I just spring the truth on her, Erich wondered, or should I lead up to it? What had happened in the upstairs bedroom wasn't easy to explain.

"Did you notice anything unusual about her?"

Sex with Batwoman was the first image to pop into his mind. "Well, she drinks. That's for sure."

"How can you tell?"

"I saw her drinking. And I could smell it on her breath."

Agent Heffernan looked up from her pad.

"You got close enough to smell her breath?"

"That's right."

He took another sip of bad coffee. Agent Heffernan slid her glasses off her nose and sat very still. Did she already know? he wondered. But how could she know? Agent Heffernan might seem bland, but maybe it was all an act.

"And?"

Erich looked straight back at her. "She took a certain interest in me."

"Oh my. Really?"

"Well, is that so surprising?"

She shrugged. "You tell me. I wasn't there. What kind of interest?"

"There was. . .unexpected proximity?"

"Don't answer me with a question, please. Spell it out."

That *was* a dumb way to put it, Erich realized. Better not get too fancy. He described how Serena Plutov had expressed displeasure at her husband's absence from Viktor's birthday party. He said she'd definitely been drinking and that she didn't seem entirely in control of her behavior. There was something needy about her. "She's—I'd guess I'd say—impulsive. That's the word."

Agent Heffernan returned to her scribbling. "You also mentioned 'unexpected proximity.' Any suggestion of physical intimacy?"

Her tone was flat. It was like someone taking his order at a pizzeria. "Extra cheese on that?" And now something in Erich revolted. She was playing with him. Suddenly this conversation felt more than personal—it was petty, bordering on mean. He pictured Serena acting bluff and tough, drinking herself into oblivion. Why talk about it out of context? Why should Agent Heffernan be privy to somebody else's misery? Serena deserved a chance to pull herself together without some stranger pawing over the embarrassing parts. He'd witnessed nothing actually criminal, and there were things in life that were nobody's business. In numerous ways, he'd already been quite serviceable to Agent Heffernan. He'd danced to her tune, in the hope that she'd throw him a nickel. But the show was over. Now, his only power with a person like her was to withhold.

"Are we finished?" he asked. "Can I leave this place and you don't call me anymore? I've done my bit with the monitors. I held up my end. You got what you wanted. I think we're finished."

All this time, Erich had been holding an unfinished donut. He gave it a big bite.

"You didn't answer my question."

"And you haven't answered mine," he retorted, chewing.

"No, we are *not* finished, Erich. Not yet. But we'll be a lot closer if you answer me."

He brushed his chin for crumbs. "About intimacy?"

She waited.

What image do you want to insert into the Shanghai Mystery Box? Will it become real?

He would have to choose his words carefully. Since intimacy, or a desperate facsimile of it, had already occurred upstairs at the Plutov house, he wasn't entirely bluffing. He had a rabbit poised and ready. But would it serve? The mystery he possessed, and could reveal—the nature of his rabbit, so to speak—ought to be obvious to anyone with open eyes and human feelings. There was *much* unhappiness in this box.

"She seems willing to look elsewhere," he said slowly.

"Do you think she'd see you again?"

Rendezvous

I? THIS IS ERICH? Just wanted to get in touch, you know. About Viktor? How is he? I hope he had a great birthday."

A pause. "*What?* Who is this?"

Erich had the distinct impression that he could hear drink in Serena's voice. More than her actual words—she'd spoken little and there was no obvious slurring—there was a slightly juicy sound that he recognized. Not a good time for his call. He was tempted to hang up, but that would be cowardly. Instead, he tried to sound jolly.

"The Amazing Ambrose? Remember me? At the party?"

"Oh, *you—*" There was a rustle and a faint whistling. Perhaps the reception was breaking up. Or was this what it sounded like when a phone was hurled across the room? Before attempting this rendezvous, Erich had been briefed by Agent Heffernan about some of the things the FBI already knew about Serena Plutov. Impulsive and erratic behavior figured among them. She was from a small town in downstate Illinois, the daughter of a soy bean wholesaler who had served on the state legislature in Springfield. In high school, Serena McKinney was her class homecoming queen and after graduation she'd come to Chicago to enroll at Loyola, where she'd competed on the varsity tennis team. She hadn't finished her degree. She'd led an active social life and had dated a relief pitcher for the White Sox and a trader at the Chicago Mercantile Exchange before marrying Andre Plutov, who was more than twenty years her senior. Aside from multiple traffic violations, Serena had no criminal record, but nine months ago she'd been forcibly removed by security guards at Bloomingdale's after an altercation in the shoe department. An obscene tirade was captured on camera, and she'd ripped down a display and caused material damage. When the store filed a criminal complaint, the Plutovs threatened a harassment lawsuit. The incident was settled out of court. Mrs. Plutov's reputation at her son's private school was one of a difficult parent who quarreled with teachers, but that information was hearsay. "We would like to know more about this person," said Agent Heffernan. "I've seen it happen before—people will have a heart-to-heart with a relative stranger. It feels safer to them. You can help us."

Now Serena's voice returned to the line, softer: "Oh, yes. Thank you for calling, Erich. I wasn't expecting it. Viktor is all right. He's doing better, though the rabbit's behavior was a bit of a shock."

"I'm *very* sorry about that."

"Oh, we know it wasn't intentional."

"It's never happened before, I swear."

"Don't worry about it. Your show made a big impression on Viktor. And I don't mean just the rabbit. He can't stop talking about it."

"Really?"

"That's right." She pitched her voice lower. "You made an impression on me, too."

Erich rubbed the side of his face. She didn't sound as if she were being ironic. He seized on her allusion, carefully choosing his next words. "You made quite an impression on *me*. I'll never look at superheroes in the same way again."

Serena laughed. "Oh, you haven't seen all my powers."

"Say, you know something?" he pursued. "I wasn't only calling about Viktor, though I'm delighted to hear that he's okay and he liked the show. I was also wondering—I've been thinking about it a lot, actually—would you like to get together again? However suits you, you name it. For instance, I've never taken a superhero out to dinner. But I'd love to, if she were available."

A pause. "Interesting. Well—all right. Let's try that."

"Wonderful!"

They chatted briefly to arrange a convenient time, and she suggested that they meet at the bar of Sasho Sensei on Thursday night. "Have you been there? You eat Japanese? It's right off Millennium Park on Washington. Easy to find. Is eight o'clock okay?"

"Sounds great. Super!"

He clicked off his phone, experiencing a jittery buzz of success. How about that! She *was* interested. His satisfaction had nothing to do with Agent Heffernan and her assignment. To hell with that. No, it was gratifying, for its own sake, to have an overture accepted by an attractive woman. Yes, it was. He smiled and pecked at his phone again, searching for information about Sasho Sensei. He'd never heard of the place but a website popped right up. He selected the menu. Holy moly! Sashimi plates started at $80. He scrolled through a tour of the restaurant, and the photos showed fountains and floating lilies.

Now he called Agent Heffernan.

"It's set up," he told her. "She's game."

"Good!"

"But I have a question about operating procedures."

"I told you, Erich, we want you as a passive contact. This meeting is just groundwork. You don't have to say or do anything in particular. Pay attention, that's all. *Listen*. And try to forget that we had this conversation. Relax like it's an ordinary night out for you."

"I can't do that."

"Why not?"

"There's something we haven't talked about."

"What?"

"Can I declare expenses?"

Brute Facts

STACI WENDALL, ERICH'S BOSS at Wendall's Original Organics, had started out as a web designer. When pregnant with her first child, she'd changed her eating habits and had been appalled by the price of kale and heirloom tomatoes. Organic strawberries cost almost as much as marijuana, which she'd recently given up. This fact was the source of her inspiration. I could grow this stuff, she thought.

In the two-car garage behind her home in Lincolnwood, she started a hydroponic garden, growing microgreens in nutrient-treated water instead of soil, under the steady glow of frequency-specific induction lights. She liked the results and soon added more trays of plantings, and then more, until the trays took over the entire space and forced their vehicles out of the garage.

Now pregnant with her third child, she'd abandoned web design and struggled to keep up with the demands of her new business, which had morphed into an urban farm. Her husband Rob, who taught at Northwestern's dental school, helped out, but it wasn't enough. That was when Erich came in. Staci and Rob were decent employers, cheerful and not too fussy about fixed hours, as long as Erich washed out the trays and readied the equipment in time for the next rotation. Deliveries, however, were different matter, respecting a strict schedule, but Staci handled most of these herself. Erich understood why, when he first accompanied her on the rounds, where they entered the service areas of posh restaurants that boasted of their fresh organic produce and saw that she was paid in envelopes of cash, which she always counted out before leaving, in order to verify the sum. Staci had a shock of premature gray hair that gave her a striking appearance, and she always wore lace-up boots as if she'd climbed down from a mountain. Restaurant managers and chefs looked on respectfully as she confirmed the total. This cash—where did it come from? Why didn't the restaurants put it on their books? The money was both a mystery and not a mystery. Of course, it was convenient for Staci's books if she were paid in cash. Much of her income wasn't declared. And whatever the legality of the transaction, the salad greens were tender and healthy, no doubt about it. Erich had developed a taste for them, and Staci and Rob kindly invited him to take home biodegradable bags of Woo party mix.

"Your health is good for everyone," Staci said, making a slow circle with her hand. "Paradigmatically, I mean. Society, and not just your probiotic digestive gut, is a holistic concern." Staci liked to talk in this way, and he quickly grasped that part of his job was to listen. She told him, "That's our real purpose here, Erich. That's the news. When we leave this world, it will make a mark in the shape of who we have been."

He nodded vigorously.

The last time Erich had spoken to Alison, she'd asked him what he was doing. "Still getting gigs? How's life treating you?"

"I'm good. I'm sober. Got a new part-time job."

"What's that?"

"I'm a hired hand at a farm."

She chuckled. "Yeah, right."

He explained about Wendall's, and they chatted in a relaxed manner. Her call was unexpected, out of the blue. She peppered him with friendly questions. Then she mentioned that she and Rodney were moving to a new apartment. Maybe that was the reason for the call, Erich thought, she wanted to share her new address. Sometimes Alison still received mail at Bonnie Kubek's duplex, and Erich forwarded it. In any event, their conversation went smoothly and there were no notes of reproach or anger. It felt as if they'd turned a page. Erich refrained from referring to Rodney Barnes as "the Perfesser," which he'd done many times earlier, to bait Alison. It had been so hard for Erich to accept that she would leave him for a man like Rodney. He was *old*. His face was perhaps handsomish, after a fashion, but Jesus, he was completely gray, he had narrow shoulders and a protruding stomach! How could Alison leave him for this Daddy Dude?

Alison was quick-witted and sexy, and Erich might've understood, though it still would've been painful, if she'd dumped him for a young guy in her crowd, some hot shot actor or a musician, say—but *freaking Rodney Barnes?* It was grotesque. Incomprehensible.

How? How? How?

For a long time, the image of Alison and Rodney was a torment to Erich. In the beginning, scratching out his own eyes wouldn't have been enough—he needed to scratch out his *brains*, to stop thinking of them together. Since that wasn't possible, he'd resorted to messing up his mind in other ways, his favorite bad excuse. His A.A. sponsor Fred Cunningham had told him that he would just have to let it go. "*Let it go! Let it go!*" Fred's face leaned in, his sad brown eyes, his crooked nose, his big chipped tooth. *"Ya hear me!"* Asking why Alison preferred to be with Rodney Barnes was like asking, Why is the sky blue? Why is water wet? Why is cold, cold? It was pointless. You couldn't interrogate brute facts of existence. You just had to accept.

Erich had begun to accept. Living by himself again, he'd gained some perspective. He'd been lucky to have her for a while, but maybe they weren't meant to be together for the long term. When they were younger, and she'd been part of Tom Denison's crowd, Alison Keating was an arty girl, an aspiring actress and dancer who wore leotards both in the studio and out. It was her uniform, she liked making an impression. Oh, she was striking. When Erich had spoken of having a child, she smiled as if accepting a compliment and then brushed it off. "We got plenty of time, there's no hurry. I've barely started my own life." Erich hadn't pressed her, and in fact he was surprised at himself, by how quickly the desire to be a father had gripped him. He couldn't explain this feeling aloud. Everything was mixed up. There was a large part of exasperation with his own upbringing, the conviction that he would do a better job than his parents who, though not ill-intentioned, had bungled the situation. He wouldn't be so sloppy—he would leave nothing to chance. There was also a measure of nostalgia: he missed his granddad Lou. He entertained a fantasy of having a son and naming him Lou. He would treat his boy with the same generosity Lou had offered him. He hadn't told Alison about this idea, not yet. Unlike himself, Alison had siblings, including elder sisters with babies. Maybe she saw her sisters' lives and wanted something else.

"Erich, I'm calling because I wanted you to hear it from me first. Rodney agrees with me. I have some special news. I'm pregnant."

The Script

ERICH HAD SAT THROUGH enough of Alison's theater performances to know that if a gun appeared in Act One, you could bet your last dollar that by the time the drama came to a close, you would hear a *bang!* He didn't like these plays very much, to tell the truth. They made him think of granddad Lou, muttering under his breath, "S.O.S."

This latest revelation from Alison, however, took him by surprise. He hadn't seen the gun before the *bang!* He hadn't even been extended the courtesy of cliché. What a disgusting shock. What a cheat!

She and Rodney were expecting a child. She and Rodney were expecting a child. She and Rodney were expecting a child.

The conversation finished, he let the phone slip from his hand and began to pace the apartment. Was he stupid to be surprised? Of course he was! Oh, the gun had been there all along, but somehow he'd been too foolish to see it. It must've been right in front of his face. What's the matter with me?

Why not *me?* Why not *me?*

He walked back and forth, sometimes speaking aloud, gesticulating. He stopped once, pressing his fingers to his face, imagining oscillating ends to his fingertips. If only he could be someone else! Transformed into what she wanted. He resumed walking.

But Alison already possessed what she wanted. And it had nothing to do with him.

And now, on his own, Erich knew what he wanted, too. He wanted to leave the apartment and go to a bar and drink himself outside of the unbearable presence of the present. Outside of time. That's where he ached to be. Away from the past and future, too. Never mind the progress he'd made. It wasn't enough. No, it wasn't enough. He had the gun.

He walked to the door, and back again. He walked to the door, and back again.

He found his phone on the floor.

"Fred, it's Erich." He exhaled a shuddering breath.

"You okay?"

"No, not at all. I'm—not okay." His words came out with a broken, jerky vehemence. "Can you come over?"

"Have you started?"

"No."

"Good! See! You done the right thing already! Now just keep on doing it, Erich, you hear me? Should I come now, or do you wanna talk some first? We can talk. Can you stay clear till I get there?"

Erich sat on the floor and clutched his knees.

"I'll try to hang on. Come over, Fred."

"On my way!"

The line went dead.

Erich didn't move, holding his knees very tightly. If he got up his legs would lead him somewhere bad. He truly didn't care, except he did, and he would. He was the sum of irreconcilable pieces.

He rolled on his side to distract his body. He brought a shirt cuff to his lips and began to suck on it, tasting the cloth. With his other hand, he clutched at his crotch.

A part of him felt ashamed. He wished he could've held it together, avoided this scene, without calling Fred. Why bother the old guy?

Or was it the knowledge that Fred was coming that allowed him to entertain such a question? Made it possible for him to stall and buy another minute? Otherwise, he would already be out of the apartment, chasing his oblivion. He'd struggled with the idea of a higher power but sometimes it helped to picture God not as an all-powerful deity on a throne but as a geezer with holes in his socks like Fred. It made a twisted kind of sense.

Erich rolled on his other side. He closed his eyes. *Oh God, please.* He was counting his breaths. Just another minute. Another minute. Fuck the gun. That script wasn't going to be *his* story.

Sasho Sensei

ERICH TOOK THE EL to Randolph/Wabash because he didn't want to worry about parking and besides, what if Serena wanted to go someplace afterward? Offering her a ride in his jeep might spoil the mood. There was a problem with his muffler and he hadn't had time to fix it. He might've borrowed the WOO van but that would look odd, too. No, it was better just to show up at the restaurant.

He arrived ten minutes early. He scouted the entrance of Sasho Sensei and continued down to the corner of State Street before turning back again, noticing his reflection in windows. He looked good. New black jeans, a crisp white shirt. Agent Heffernan had told him he couldn't declare clothes as expenses but he'd bought them anyway, for his own pleasure. He touched his hair, pressed at his cowlick, smoothing it back. (He'd never gotten used to gel.) Heffernan had allotted up to $160 for the dinner. "That's upper end with us, I'll have you know," she'd told him. "And don't think you have to spend it all. Let her pay her half. Believe me, Serena Plutov can afford it."

Erich was also wearing his favorite black boots. They'd been made in Spain and he'd bought them years ago because he liked their bold simplicity—like a cowboy boot, but with a round toe and without garish stitching or contrasting colors. It had taken a long time to break them in, but now the boots were supple, even springy, nestling perfectly with the form of his feet. He could've worn them to bed, they fit so comfortably. They also made him taller.

He didn't want Serena to find him gawking like a tourist in front of the restaurant, so he went inside. Five minutes early was no big deal. If she was late, he could always watch the ballgame at the bar.

"Well *hello!*"

Serena was already there, perched on a barstool, her long legs crossed, one sandal dangling at the end of her toe.

"Hi," he said.

"Get over here!"

She slid her glass. "I'll take another," she said to a barman in black monogrammed blouse. "Ambrose, what are you having?"

"Club soda, please. Twist of lime."

"Oh, that's right," she said. "You're a Mormon now. Was it inconsiderate of me to suggest this place? Sorry! Maybe you're not happy here."

"It's fine. Really."

She leaned on one elbow as if to appraise him from another angle. "Well. . .don't forget your options! If you change your mind and want a drink, just for old time's sake, I won't tattle on you." She laughed and brought a finger to her lips. "*Shhhhh.*"

Erich didn't return the laugh. Some jokes weren't amusing, and he wasn't going to pretend they were.

"I'm okay."

He climbed onto a barstool, hearing plunking strings and a bone-like rattle of traditional Japanese music. This wasn't the kind of place, he realized, for a TV and a ballgame.

"Thank you for inquiring about Viktor," she said. "That was sweet of you. He's doing well."

"Glad to hear it."

The barman put down the drinks and she turned on her stool, recrossing her legs. "That looks like a new shirt." She reached out and fingered the material. "Nice. Tell me, Ambrose, how does a person get to be a *magician?* I've always wanted to know."

Erich fiddled with his straw. Was she mocking him? Her hand left his shirt, then came back to poke him on the chest.

"It's in the family. We've been at this for a long time." Erich had no desire to tell his story but he briefly explained his background.

"Oh, so you're following in your daddy's footsteps. Wonderful!"

"Something like that."

Strings plunked; bones rattled.

He added, "And yourself? How does someone become—you?"

She lowered her glass.

"What's that supposed to mean? You think you really know about me?"

"No, not at all. That's why I'm asking."

He had the impression that his refusal of alcohol was irksome to her, like a reminder or a reproach. If Agent Heffernan thought Serena needed a heart-to-heart, it probably wasn't going to be about her husband and the kind of business that interested the FBI. Still, what she said next surprised him.

"Ambrose, the main thing you need to know about me is that I'm a mom."

She took another sip. There was a silence. He looked at her in the bar mirror, where he saw that she was looking at him. She didn't avert her gaze when he met her eyes.

Eventually she murmured, "You hungry, Ambrose?"

"Sure."

"I'm not so hungry myself." She pushed away her empty glass.

You'd better eat something, he thought. You've got a load on.

"We could go somewhere else," she said. "Where there aren't so many people. Isn't that what this is about? Meeting up like this. Don't pretend with me. What do you say?" She reached out and tapped his knee, a smile playing on her lips. "Actually, I won't be denied."

"Well. . .all right."

Serena opened her purse and dropped three twenties on the bar. "Let me get this." She slid off her stool, grabbing his arm for balance. "Come on. I'm parked out back."

Erich moved ahead of her to push open the door. The parking lot at Sasho Sensei's was behind the building, a tight row with room for barely a dozen cars. Serena stopped in front of a silver Audi and fumbled in her purse for keys. "I can drive," Erich suggested. "Really, I don't mind."

"Give me a second."

She seemed absorbed, and then Erich noticed a large man in a tie-dye T-shirt at the end of the row. He walked purposefully in their direction. Serena didn't look up and Erich thought, Careful! If she didn't pay attention, she could get her purse snatched. Erich stepped around, putting himself in front of her. Serena looked up, and then said to the approaching man, "He's the one."

"Come here, sweetheart," the man said.

"What?" Erich asked.

Now he heard quick footsteps behind him, and glanced over his shoulder. There was another man, advancing with a baseball bat.

The car chirped, Serena moved toward it. "You hurt my son, asshole! That makes you *laugh*? It's not funny. You think I'm a joke? Let's hear you laugh now."

A quick glance in both directions: there was nowhere to go which wasn't blocked by one of the men. "Bye, Ambrose!" Serena climbed into her front seat. The man with the bat broke into a run and Erich didn't have time to think. He wasn't conscious of making a decision, but since neither direction offered an outlet, he invented a third. He ran straight at a parked car and leaped on the trunk and scrabbled onto its roof.

The men hurried after him, converging on either side of the car, but Erich jumped onto the roof of the next car, and when they followed, the next. Serena's engine roared to life and she backed out of her space. Tires squealed as she sped out of the parking lot, her car bouncing into the street.

"Get down, fuckface!"

Erich hopped to the roof of another car, momentarily slipped but regained his footing. Serena's exit had left a gap in the row of cars, which was bad news, because he couldn't go too far in that direction without being cornered. He feinted, then hopped back. The men cursed and followed. The man with the bat surged with surprising swiftness and took a swipe at Erich's shins.

Erich jumped, the bat missed. The man swung again, and once more Erich jumped. The man panted. "Come on, motherfucker." The height of the car gave the man a bad angle for his swings and now Erich turned and jumped to another car. He cast a fleeting look at the wall abutting the parking lot, the yellow bricks of the adjoining building. There was a line of ventilator ducts and a fire escape, but both were out of reach. He couldn't jump that high.

Boom!

The bat crashed on the car roof, narrowly missing his ankles. *Boom! Boom!* He had to watch the bat man closely, to anticipate his next swing, but then he felt a tug behind him, as the man in the tie-dye T-shirt managed to get closer and grab at his feet. "Sweetheart!" he shouted. Erich spun around and kicked viciously at the man's face, but he didn't connect. Then he spun again and jumped to stay clear of the bat. The hands kept clutching behind him. With his next jump, he landed unevenly and was thrown off balance, whereupon he stamped a crazy dance to regain his footing. A *scream*—his boot heel had come squarely down on the tie-dye man's fingers. Then Erich leaped just in time to evade another swing of the bat.

"That's my car! Stop it!"

A stranger in a blue sports jacket stood at the end of the row. No doubt another customer from Sasho Sensei. He pulled out a cell phone and began to punch a number.

"Put that phone down!" shouted the man with the bat, while the fellow with tie-dye T-shirt staggered a half circle in the parking lot lane, clutching his hand in front of him, groaning and cursing. He dropped to his knees. "Put it down!" shouted the man with the bat.

"Fuck you." The man in the blue sports jacket clapped his phone to his ear. "Yes, I'm calling to report—"

The man with the bat charged, and a look of horror came over the caller. He turned and fled for the street. His pursuer was closing fast, but Erich didn't wait to watch the rest. He leaped to the ground as the groaning man in the tie-dye T-shirt turned around. Erich sprinted past him. Ahead, he glimpsed the man with the bat turning right, in his pursuit of the caller, so Erich exited the lot to the left, darting between pedestrians, pounding the pavement.

Hired Hands

"HOW DID IT GO?" Agent Heffernan asked.

Oh, he'd give her an earful—but where to begin? It wasn't just the fact of being attacked, though that was bad enough. He'd tell her all about *that*. But there were other things that she couldn't begin to understand or appreciate, details that entered the picture. It might not seem like much to her that his new white shirt was ripped under one sleeve. He couldn't remember when the rip had occurred, maybe when he'd jumped down from the car to flee. But there it was, the shirt was ruined, and he'd worn it only once. Worse still, back at his apartment in Rogers Park, wearily tugging off his boots, he'd discovered—*ooh, disgusting!*—a bloody fingernail clinging to the back of one heel. Now that was really nasty. Ack!

He picked off the fingernail with a tissue and threw it in the trash receptacle in his bathroom; an hour later, unable to shake the image from his mind, he went to the bathroom and tied up the plastic bag and carried it out to the dumpster. In a weird way, this gesture wasn't only for his own comfort. It was out of respect for Bonnie Kubek. Her duplex wasn't supposed to be the kind of place where you had such things. He felt angry with Agent Heffernan. She hadn't warned him of such bullshit. It wasn't part of the deal.

Sitting in her office at FBI regional headquarters, Erich rubbed his hands on the front of his pants and described what had happened at Sasho Sensei, and how he'd made his escape from the parking lot.

"Oh, I'm so sorry," said Agent Heffernan. "I'm just as surprised as you are. At least you're okay, right?"

"Just peachy. For Christ's sake. Whatever."

She made him tell his story again, and Erich didn't hide his irritation when they started a third time. But that was the protocol, and she wasn't happy when he mentioned Serena's parting words, her allusion to Viktor's injury from the rabbit at the party. "You didn't tell me about that before! Why not? You should have!" She also let him know that the fingernail on his boot heel could've provided useful DNA evidence, if he'd saved it and brought it to her. "Just to confirm," she said, "One of those guys in the parking lot called you 'Sweetheart?' You're sure about that?"

"Yeah. But the guy with the bat was my big worry. I had to keep an eye on him. He was trying to whack me. The other guy was behind me most of the time."

"Answer me quickly: what was the color of his hair?"

"Uh. . ." Erich tried to picture him but he saw mainly a tie-dye T-shirt. Broad shoulders, a large belly. His face, though, was a blank. How was he supposed to remember such details? "Brownish hair, I think. Pretty long, going down both sides of his face."

"What about his face? Any distinguishing features?"

"Not really. It happened fast, you know? He was fairly big, I can tell you that. Like the guy with the bat."

Erich noticed that Agent Heffernan had stopped taking notes. It left him with an impression that his account wasn't good enough, he was letting her down. Not pulling his weight. But that seemed crazy, after what he'd been through.

"You have to stay away from those guys," she said.

"Oh *really?* Ya think?"

"Don't be annoyed, please. You have every reason to be upset by this experience but we have to anticipate. You can't let the emotions cloud your judgment of the future."

"It's not like I sought these guys out. It's Serena. She set it up. She's a drunk and she's fucking nuts and she's violent. She has no limits."

"I hear you," Agent Heffernan said, "but there's a context. That's all I mean."

"Like, it's justified from their side? You got to be kidding."

"No, no. A context for future *caution.*"

She assumed a confidential tone which he recognized from earlier conversations, when she told him something that he was supposed to appreciate as a favor, but that he didn't want to hear.

"I can't comment on ongoing cases," she said. "But I want to help. Your description doesn't give me much to go on, I would barely call it a description. But if we can link Serena to these men, we will. Andre Plutov's associates are no strangers to such people. But hired hands don't work for free. To pay for such services, Serena has to have a reason."

Muscles tightened on the back of Erich's neck. "She doesn't even know me!"

"She already gave you one reason, didn't she? She's getting even for what you did to her son."

"So you think that's possible. For a *rabbit*. An accident!"

"Don't raise your voice with me. I'm not defending her. But you should've told me about it earlier, not held anything back. It might seem absurd but consider how a lawyer would spin it. You were responsible for an initial injury, which was aggravated by humiliation. You caused a mother to snap. She's standing up for her child. People lose all sense of perspective. They take desperate measures. Is there anything else you're not telling me?"

"Like, we also had sex at her son's birthday party?"

"Oh stop it, that's not even funny. I have to be able to trust you, Erich. You've seen what you're up against. That's why I'm telling you to keep low. No more contact with Serena Plutov. I won't ask anything more of you."

"And the charges? There will be no charges filed against me?"

She was much too slow to answer. "I'm absolutely in favor of that, Erich. But it's not my final decision."

"So you've been stringing me along, all this time. I risk my neck for nothing!"

"No. That's not fair."

"You've threatened me with jail, and I haven't done jack-shit. I wouldn't call that fair."

"I repeat: I won't ask anything more of you. But stay in touch, okay, if someone approaches you. Keep me informed."

The Room

GRANDDAD LOU HAD WARNED HIM against dealings with the mob. In Lou's day it had been a different mob, but if he were still alive, Erich knew what he would say. "You're always a mark with those people. Leave the room. There's no making nice or being neutral. *Leave the goddamn room.* That's all you can do. It might appear that someone else is the mark and that might even be true but at the same time, you're still a mark, too. *Leave the room.*"

Erich had witnessed Lou cut short a conversation at Schaefer's Tavern and disappear into the kitchen when certain strangers walked in the door. He never understood how his grandfather recognized them, but these customers got waited on by part-timers. Lou was always too busy. He'd even seen his grandfather interrupt a performance in the middle of a routine and sweep up his close-up pad, saying he'd be back later, because he had an errand. Lou practiced what he preached. He left the room.

One night, after closing time, his granddad told Erich a story. *"I'm not proud of this, but this is what happened. . ."*

While he was in the navy, Lou had accepted work dealing crooked poker on the south side. He'd expected to be sent over to Europe but he'd passed an examination and was assigned to radio and radar training at Great Lakes Naval Station, just north of the city. The war ended while he was still taking his course, so he remained stateside, waiting to be demobilized. He lived on base and was able to get weekend passes and free baseball tickets to Wrigley from the USO. It was a sweet arrangement. Immense good luck. He was usually home for Sunday dinner with his mother. At the USO, he met a fellow who knew of his reputation as a card handler, and this fellow offered him some work for Saturday nights.

"They're running a game at the Hotel Biltmore, you got guys from all over, going in and out. You deal to third base. Low but steady. Wear your uniform, too, that makes a good impression. The rest will take care of itself."

Lou knew of such arrangements. A dealer at a crooked table discreetly ensured that the third person from his left got a break on good cards. Never a spectacular hand—that would be harder to set up, and would attract notice—but an edge in the odds from a dealer culling high value cards or dealing

dreck to other players. A confederate to the right of the dealer would coop-
erate when it was his turn to cut the deck at the beginning of a hand, by ca-
sually cutting to a crimp. A good card handler could make a nearly invisible
crimp.

Thus the three or four other players at the table were consistently disad-
vantaged. There were no cold deck switches or anything fancy or risky. Lou
just culled and crimped with workmanlike competence. Over the course of
a long poker night—sometimes these games lasted till dawn—the cumulative
effect would tell. The person on third base would leave the table a winner.
And, as a rule, this person was a stranger to the premises, who would never
set foot in the Biltmore again. The real beneficiary was a regular at the table
who'd spent the evening cutting to the crimp, maybe even losing, modestly,
not attracting attention to himself. He was the fixer, and the fixer would
meet with the winner after the game and take 60% of the receipts, as pre-
agreed. A very respectable profit.

Granddad Lou started dealing to third base on Saturday nights, in return for which he received a cash cut, too, which he spent on flowers or nice
beefsteaks for his mother the following Sunday. When he dealt, the fixer ignored him, and Lou did his best not to notice him, either. The best policy
was to forget the accomplice was there.

But one night, toward eleven o'clock, he had the impression that the
fixer was watching him closely, with a distinct air of irritation. Lou ignored
him, but by one o'clock that morning it was unmistakable, a grimace, or
even a sneer as the man threw in his ante. Maybe the guy was drunk—they
were all having bourbon. Lou kept his head down and continued dealing to
third base, to a jug-eared kid in his army uniform who crowed with delight
when he won a big pot. This, too, was unusual, and ill-advised. A soldier
on third base didn't surprise him, because guys like that would ship out of
town and be conveniently out of the way if anybody asked questions; they
were often recruited at a nearby whorehouse. But this soldier's manner was
inappropriate, talking loud. Worse, he called attention to Lou, ribbing him
about his navy uniform, at one point even exclaiming, "I didn't know you
navy boys liked me so much! Keep those good cards comin'!" He was drunk,
totally forgetting himself.

The game broke up after two o'clock, and Lou went down to the hotel
kitchen to collect his cut. Two angry men awaited him.

"Fuck is wrong with you? What were you doing?"

Lou didn't understand. "I did my job."

"But you were dealing to third base all night. Don't lie to us! You must've been."

"Sure I was," Lou said. "Of course I was!"

The men looked at each other, and their faces sagged. Eventually the shorter one, a squat fellow everybody called Fireplug Stan, said, "You didn't get the word, did you?"

"Huh?"

"You were supposed to deal to second base tonight. We mix it up sometimes, keep things rotating. You just cost us three hundred dollars, you idiot."

"But that's not my fault!"

"We have to get that money back."

They wouldn't listen to him, and it became clear that as far as they were concerned, Lou owed them. Never mind his excuse, he'd handed over money to a stranger. That fact was not going to go away.

"We need you here on Friday nights, too," said Fireplug Stan. "Got that? Next week, it'll be Friday and Saturday."

"But I can't do that! I can't get permission for both nights."

"Say you got somebody sick in your family. Figure it out. Whatever. Friday *and* Saturday."

"It's not that simple!"

"You got three hundred bucks?" Stan asked.

"No, I don't."

"Enough of this shit. See you Friday and Saturday."

After this unpleasant conversation, Lou decided to lie low. He was convinced that he didn't owe them $300. He also suspected that the drunken soldier who'd left the Biltmore Hotel that night didn't make it home unscathed; the money was probably already recovered. But Lou didn't want to know the details. He didn't ask for a permission the following weekend. He stayed at the naval station on Friday and Saturday nights and listened to the radio and joked around with some guys in his unit who'd been grounded for disciplinary reasons. They weren't the smartest guys but it was actually relaxing. He sent a telegram to his mother that he wouldn't be home for Sunday dinner.

Nobody can touch me here, he thought. Fireplug Stan can fuck off.

So he was surprised when, the following Wednesday, Lieutenant Michaels took him aside and said, "You asked for your permission yet?"

Lieutenant Michaels had never spoken to Lou before. He was like a passing breeze when Lou stood at attention and the Lieutenant walked by.

"Sir? My permission, sir?"

"Friend at the USO was asking about you. We've penciled you in for Friday and Saturday. You just need to do the paperwork."

"Sir, yes sir."

He couldn't believe it. Now he had no choice. He seriously doubted that Lieutenant Michaels cared about a card game on the south side, but clearly there was something else, something that mattered to him, that pushed him to do Fireplug Stan's bidding. Did *this officer* owe those guys a favor? Permissions were jealously monitored. You couldn't take them for granted. A soldier got permission for Friday or Saturday, but not both. For Lou to get a permission for both nights meant that somebody else was denied, for his sake. It was embarrassing.

He'd thought that he was safe at the naval station, behind a wall. But no, that wall was an illusion.

Lou did as he was told. He reported to the Biltmore on Friday and was assigned a table. Two minutes before the game started, Fireplug Stan appeared at the door, waving for him to come over.

Lou approached and Stan handed him a clean ashtray, a pretext in case anyone was watching them. He leaned in close. "First base this time, Einstein." Then he turned away.

Lou walked back to the table, his neck flushed. He'd never worked as an ashtray boy before. An added insult. He put it on the table and the game began and he dealt the cards. All the while, his disgust grew. Some unsuspecting soldier back at the naval station had been denied permission in order for Lou to do *this*. He pictured a lonely kid who needed a night out, stewing in the barracks. Lou also looked closely at the players around the card table, the ones unaware of the fix. On other nights he'd been uncurious; he'd considered them as run-of-the-mill suckers. They were asking for it if they came to a place like this.

But tonight everything was different. One player in particular troubled Lou—a seedy old guy in a straw hat. He needed a shave, and he was over-polite, calling everybody Mister. At the sight of Lou's uniform, he started telling stories of serving in Belgium and France during the Great War. He asked Lou about himself, and Lou admitted that he hadn't been sent over. This old guy looked like a bum and he wasn't even drinking. Maybe he couldn't afford it. Lou imagined him in financial straits, desperate for a few dollars, foolishly thinking he might improve his situation at a card table. The fellow was cleaned out before midnight.

On Saturday, Lou didn't show up to deal cards at the Biltmore. He was still on permission, so he went to the movies on Lake Street. But he couldn't concentrate on the picture, unable to forget the bum he'd cheated. Lou didn't visit his mother the next day for Sunday dinner. He was eager to return to the naval station.

Oh, he knew that it wouldn't be easy to get away. They would come looking for him. His problem, he grasped, was more than a question of three hundred dollars. They saw him as a larger investment. He would have to be smart.

"But you're crazy!" an ensign told him the following Monday when he volunteered for re-assignment at a technical training facility in Millington, Tennessee. "You'd be way out in the sticks, nowhere near Chicago. Know what that place is famous for? Mosquitoes!"

"Just help me with the papers," Lou said. "Where do I sign?"

An Invitation for Mr. Boots

TWO NIGHTS AFTER HIS LAST INTERVIEW with Agent Heffernan, Erich's phone rang after he'd gone to bed. He snapped awake, his mind racing, not bleary at all. It was as if he'd been expecting this call.

He couldn't put his finger on *what* exactly he'd been expecting, but somehow he was ready. Not so long ago he might've worried that a call at this hour concerned his mother in Florida. Maybe there'd been an accident, or a heart attack. She and her husband Brice had ballooned in weight and sometimes they injured their knees just by trying to walk. Or, he might've hoped it was Alison. Tearfully telling him that she'd made a big mistake, she was sorry, it had been a temporary bout of insanity to run off with Professor Barnes but now she knew where she belonged, and that was by his side. Would he forgive her? Would he take her back? Please, oh please. . .

Erich coughed to clear his voice. "Hello? Yes?"

Silence.

He repeated, "Hello?"

A raspy laugh.

"I got an idea about your rabbit! It came to me in a dream and it's *perfect.*"

"My rabbit?"

No introduction was necessary: he recognized Serena's voice.

"Yes, your bunny-wunny," she said. "When I was a kid, you see, I was in 4-H."

Erich waited. "What do you mean?"

"You don't know about 4-H? Such a city boy! You have some learning to do. 'Head, Heart, Hands and Health.' When you grow up in the country it's a fun organization. Kids get together for after-school programs and crafts and parties. When you're older, you organize dances. Ride horses. You learn skills! For instance, I can skin a rabbit. Did you know that? This is going to be interesting, Ambrose."

The line went silent.

Bonkers! he thought. He turned on a light and got up. He went to the bathroom and then, instead of returning to bed, he sat in a chair and stared at the digital clock on his TV. It said 2:32 a.m. She was calling him—at home!—at this hour. Okay, right, she had his number from booking the birthday party. Right. But his address? Had she figured that out? Did she know where he lived? He no longer had a land line and wasn't in the directories, but it probably wasn't hard to discover by other means. Would she tell her hired hands where he lived?

"*Come here, sweetheart.*"

"*Sorry! I didn't mean to break your fingers!*"

Erich sprang out of his chair and checked the lock on his door. The downstairs entrance was closed, too, he was sure. Not that these modest measures would dissuade a professional. Granddad Lou had said that a person should leave the room. But what if the room was your own freaking house?

He retrieved his wallet and fished out Agent Heffernan's card and called her number. Of course he got her voicemail, at this hour.

"Erich Ambrose here. I need your help. I've just received a threat from Serena Plutov." He took a breath. "This occurred at my home. I'm counting on your support."

There. She would find the message first thing tomorrow morning. *This* morning, he wearily corrected himself.

He turned out the lights and walked around his apartment in the dark, peering from his windows to the street below, and then on the other side, to the back yard and the rise of train tracks. He swore under his breath and returned to bed.

Erich woke up at dawn on his couch, and he couldn't remember leaving his bed to seek somewhere else. Skin my rabbit? he thought. I don't even have a rabbit.

The King of Spain

"**Y**OU'RE LATE," said Staci Wendall.

"Sorry. I had an appointment downtown and it took longer than I thought."

Erich finished hosing a tray and in his haste, he splashed his jeans and shoes. Water soaked into his sock, and he involuntarily shivered.

"It's not the first time," she reminded him. "I've got to pick up the kids. So I'll have to finish this tonight when they're home. The point is, Erich, when I said we could be flexible about your hours, it wasn't supposed to encroach on the family. On the *children*. Do you think we'd be better off with a time clock? Should I require you to punch in? Because I've never seen our relationship that way. To be honest."

Erich kept his head down and reached for another tray. True, on another occasion he'd been late due to negligence; he'd lost track of the hour and then got caught in traffic. But this time was different, because he'd been at FBI regional headquarters with Agent Heffernan. Erich definitely had his reasons. But he couldn't explain all this to Staci.

"I'm sorry," he repeated.

"Yes, I heard you." She stood by him, rubbing a light circle on her stomach, first one direction then another. She was now five months pregnant. Erich realized that she was waiting for him to say more. His apology wasn't good enough. She saw him in a different light now. But. . .well, the feeling was mutual! Earlier he'd liked Staci, and perhaps he'd been unduly flattered when she and Rob took interest in his sleight of hand career. They thought it was hip and original and in keeping with the indie image of WOO. "Yours is an under-appreciated performance art," Rob said. "In our way, this business and the new food paradigm are attempting a similar alteration of perceptions." Erich wasn't sure what this meant, beyond the jolly suggestion that they would all be artists together. Very nice! But now Staci hovered and let him know that he'd encroached on the sacred hoop of the family. On the *children*. Erich suppressed a sigh.

He reached for another tray. Staci didn't budge. He fantasized turning the hose on her, to drive her away, but eventually he managed: "It won't happen again. I'll do some soul-searching."

This seemed to satisfy her, and she left him to his work.

His conversation with Agent Heffernan that morning hadn't gone any better. Today she wore a powder-blue tracksuit, as if she'd come straight to her desk from the gym—or maybe she was on her way there, since she didn't appear flushed. He recounted Serena's threat and Heffernan was quick to shift the responsibility for the problem.

"If you'd told me about the rabbit attacking her child the first time around, all this could've been avoided. I would never have sent you out. Obviously she doesn't like you or your rabbit."

"Boots."

"What?"

"His name is Boots."

"Fine."

"Actually, it's Mr. Boots."

"Would you cut the crap?"

Erich held his ground. "I've already been assaulted once, right? And it's not over. She's seeking me out. Not letting it go. I need protection."

"Do you have a gun?"

"No, that's not what I meant. There's—"

"You might consider availing yourself of this right, it could be a smart thing. But not in haste. I wouldn't advise anyone untrained or unlicensed to get a gun. You need to proceed prudently. You should take a course."

"You're not listening to me!"

They went back and forth, and Agent Heffernan told him that it was too early to bring in Serena for questioning. "If we approach her now it would start a roadblock of lawyers. Everybody runs for cover. We've got no I.D.s on the assailants. They could be out of town by now. Out of state. We're still following up on your story."

"Till you know, I need police protection."

"What are you, the King of Spain? You want a personal security detail? You have any idea how much that costs? Listen, I'm not saying I don't believe you. But that's not the way it works. The thing now is to be *smart*. Keep your eyes open. Lie low for a while, go to a motel. Don't you have friends you can stay with for a few nights?"

"Well, sure. But I don't see that as a solution."

"For now, it's the best we can do. Trust me."

The Denisons

WHERE DO YOU GO when you're supposed to avoid your own home? Erich had answered Agent Heffernan's question about friends without hesitation, but in truth it wasn't that straightforward. Sure, he had friends. He wasn't some hermit. But when you're almost thirty, it wasn't as simple as it used to be.

You just couldn't call up a buddy and crash on his couch, not like in the old days. Now your buddy was married and was dealing with his toddler who had the flu. Or he'd taken a job out of town. Some friends still shared their apartments, so you'd be imposing on roommates, creating a situation with strangers. And never mind your ex. Oh sure, he could just imagine sitting down for spaghetti with Alison and the Perfesser. Old Rodney Barnes smiling at him, wearing a foulard around his neck and gripping a cheese grater. "Some parmesan with that, Erich?"

No fucking thanks. Besides, this time of year, Alison and the Perfesser worked at their summer theater retreat, a place in the woods called "Embrace Your Aesthetic." A sort of indoctrination camp for the *ahhts*, with inspirational talks around bonfires and other horrors. So where did that leave him? No point in bothering mutual friends of Alison. (He didn't want word to get back to her that he was in some kind of trouble and lacked a place to stay.) There was a woman named Loretta that he'd slept with a few times in the wake of his divorce, and she'd left a friendly voicemail barely two weeks ago, but he hadn't responded, because Loretta always wanted to get high and did he really want to put himself in those situations again? Of course there was always Fred Cunningham. With Fred, he wouldn't even have to call in advance. He could show up drunk or bleeding at his doorstep and Fred would take him in. Fred was God, the bosom of Abraham. But the old guy's apartment was so tiny and depressing, smelling of ancient undershirts and mentholated cough drops and canned beef stew, with a TV always blaring. Did he *want* to go?

Erich felt a twinge of guilt. It had been a long time since he'd paid Fred a proper social call. Support went two ways, and Erich hadn't been holding up his end. He should invite Fred to breakfast, get him out of his apartment. The last time they'd gone to Thurston's, Fred had enjoyed it very much, even flirted with the waitress, in a jokingly Bad Fred kind of way. ("Bad Fred" was how Fred referred to his behavior in the days before he got sober, in tales of stealing his sister's credit cards or selling her medication on the street, or waking up in a Laredo jail cell with a broken collar-bone and two black eyes.) Yes, he should invite Fred for breakfast. . .one of these days.

But today, his choice was obvious. He would call Tom Denison. He'd already confided in Tom about his recent troubles, so his request wouldn't require a lot of extra explaining. True, Tom had moved in with his parents, but Erich had known the family for years, and Tom's parents had always been kind.

"Well. . .sure," Tom answered slowly, when Erich called him at work. "I'll confirm with Mom and get back to you."

"Sorry. It's short notice."

A pause. "It's not that. But it's Wednesday. And at our house that's *Monopoly* night. We play every Wednesday. You wouldn't mind playing *Monopoly?*"

"Of course not."

"All right then." Tom sounded relieved.

Arrangements were made, and Erich's jeep rolled up to the curb at the appointed time in front of a creamy two-story house with trimmed hedge. Mrs. Denison greeted him at the door and invited him to take off his shoes and put on a pair of guest slippers. Mr. Denison shook his hand warmly. "My man!" He finished his handshake with a confidential pat on the shoulder. Erich remembered vividly an incident when he was sixteen years old, when he stayed over at the Denisons' house one night and the next morning he'd accidently witnessed Tom Senior standing in the kitchen in his bathrobe in front of the open refrigerator, licking a stick of butter. His tongue moved with long, catlike strokes. Erich had stood by and watched him, fascinated. Tom Senior put the butter dish back in the refrigerator and closed the door, whereupon he turned and discovered Erich. Startled, he drew up his shoulders. "You didn't see that," he said, and briskly walked away.

For dinner, there was lasagna. "Tom, will you stir the salad?" Young Tom still wore his white shirt and dress pants from work and he carefully turned the leaves so as not to spot his clothes with oil. Tonight Erich felt a difference that he hadn't fully appreciated in the old days. Sure, when they were kids, it was already obvious that the Denisons had more money than the Ambroses; Tom's father was a physical therapist, his mother was an administrator for a health corporation. But it didn't matter because he and Tom were pals who saw the world in similar ways and listened to the same music and laughed at the same jokes. Differences of class and money had seemed mere accidents. Erich took his cues from granddad Lou, who at Schaefer's Tavern engaged the company of anybody of his choosing; at the bar, everyone, including politicians and the rich and famous, was his equal; Erich had seen this with his own eyes and didn't question its general applicability. But now, watching Tom stir the salad, it came home to him how much Tom resembled his parents, while those youthful diversions and enthusiasms that had seemed so important and personally defining when they were growing up, might not add up to much.

"Are you happy with your decorator?" Mrs. Denison asked.

In order to avoid the subject of the FBI, Tom had told his parents that Erich was staying over because his apartment was freshly repainted.

"Yes, just fine."

"We can recommend some good people for you," said Mr. Denison. "We re-did the bathrooms and boy, are we tickled."

"Tom has a new bedroom set, too," she said. "Picked it out yourself, didn't you, kiddo?"

"Mmmh," said Tom.

Soon the conversation shifted to earlier days.

"Remember Tom as Biff Loman?" his mother asked. "He was great in *Death of a Salesman*."

"Terrific," said his father.

Tom ducked his head and chewed.

Erich nodded. "Sure. I remember that one very well."

Alison had had a minor role in the same show, playing a secretary, wearing a 1940s style pencil dress that suited her perfectly. The image was imprinted on Erich's brain, a hieroglyph of early love, impossible to erase.

"I always liked Tom's musicals best," Mrs. Denison continued, beaming. "You were ten years old, eleven maybe, and you used to stand beside the TV during *The Sound of Music* and sing along with the Captain von Trapp? You put on that little green Tyrolean jacket?"

Erich thought Tom might tell his mother to ease up, but he swallowed a mouthful of lasagna and intoned,

"*Edelweiss, Edelweiss,*
Every morning you greet me.

Small and white, clean and bright
You look happy to meet me."

His parents moved their heads in time with the rhythm. Erich blinked, not sure that he should be witnessing this. It was like walking into a room and discovering them naked, bodies painted, performing a ritual with a small goat. There were mysteries, things difficult to fathom that were none of his business. He recalled how Alison had asked him if Tom was closeted gay. Girls thought he was cute and even chased after him but he never stuck with one for very long. As far as Erich could tell, Tom had never seemed particularly concerned by sex, one way or another. He liked to play roles. He was self-contained. So, it seemed, was the family.

Dinner was followed by *Monopoly*. Tom led Erich to the rec room and set out the board and bank. "You sure you don't mind?"

"Sure. Haven't played in a million years, but why not?"

"It's like a tournament," Tom said. "We keep track of results from week to week."

Erich laughed. "Well, I won't get my hopes up about winning."

"It doesn't matter," Tom said. "A fourth player changes the dynamic so probably we won't count tonight's game toward the tournament results. We won't mark it on the chart."

Erich waited a moment. "You have a *chart?*"

"Yeah. Makes it easier when we do the seeds for the play-offs."

Before his parents joined them, Tom pointed to the various *Monopoly* tokens, the hat, the wheelbarrow and the ship, and asked, if Erich didn't mind, for him not to choose the little dog, because that was his mother's favorite piece and she was superstitious about it. Erich agreed, and spent the next two hours navigating his ship across properties and in and out of jail, before going bankrupt. In the end, Tom and his little hat emerged victorious.

When it was time to retire, Tom showed him his room and handed him a towel and said confidentially, "Use the Wi-Fi if you like, there's no password, but don't watch any porn, okay, because I happen to know that Mom set a browser mousetrap."

Erich clutched his towel.

"Don't look at me like that," Tom added. "It's nothing personal."

"I don't even understand what you said."

"Well, she caught Dad watching porn and she's bought a filter on our system that will monitor what pages get viewed in this house. If you watch something, Dad might get blamed. Giving you a heads up, that's all. Good night."

The following morning, the Denisons insisted that he join them for breakfast. Erich had the impression that they didn't ordinarily sit down for this meal together, as there was some confusion in the kitchen, but the family made an effort for him. Mrs. Denison offered eggs; Tom squeezed out fresh orange juice; Tom Senior was in charge of toast.

"You're welcome to stay with us tonight, Erich," said Mrs. Denison. "This is movie night. We're doing a Bette Davis retrospective. We'll send out for pizza."

"Thank you, but I need to get back to my place. Now that it's all spiffy."

Mr. Denison pointed to the toast. "You want some butter on that, Erich?"

Trashed

RIVING AWAY FROM THE DENISONS' quiet street, Erich decided to go straight home. He wouldn't look for a motel. Just because Serena Plutov had babbled some goofy bullshit didn't mean he should retreat to the Denisons' bubble. It was important to keep a sense of perspective. He didn't regret reporting Serena to Agent Heffernan, but he didn't want to follow her down a rabbit hole. You heard someone talking crazy, and if you weren't careful it rubbed off and you began to participate in the delusion. His own home was where he belonged. When Erich reached his street, the familiarity of the patch of grass and broken sidewalk in front of Bonnie Kubek's duplex looked inviting. He felt as if he'd been away for longer than one night.

He climbed the stairs and unlocked his front door and after two steps, he froze.

Upturned chairs. Tipped shelves. Books and papers were strewn on the floor. For long seconds he did not move.

He inspected the lock. No sign of tampering. Gingerly he walked around heaps in the living room that included pieces of granddad Lou's old magic library. Its out-of-print volumes and crudely stapled mimeographed pamphlets were perhaps a treasure appreciated only by sleight of hand aficionados, but they were a treasure nonetheless. Anger streaked through him. It wasn't only a break-in at his apartment. Someone had trashed his family.

In the kitchen he found a broken window by the fire escape, which explained the entrance. In the bedroom, drawers had been dumped out. He noticed a pile of cash on his dresser, where he'd thrown his customer tips from his table-to-table performance at the Althea Dinner Theater. Mainly ones and fives, not a huge sum of money but, as far as he could tell, it was untouched. He saw his laptop, too. Undisturbed.

He called Agent Heffernan.

"Looks like you were right. I had visitors."

She told him she was busy now but he could stop by her office in the afternoon. This irritated him, but he had no choice, so he reported to work at Wendall's Original Organics, dispatched his tasks for Staci, and then made the trip downtown to the regional headquarters.

"I've got some news," Heffernan announced. "We've checked out the incident in the Sasho Sensei parking lot. A criminal complaint has been filed by the owner of one of the cars. Sounds like it was the fellow who got chased away. In the complaint he says there were three vandals. Two on the ground, and one jumping up and down on his car. I suppose that was you."

"Yes, but—"

"Eye witnesses are often unreliable. The man was scared. The other two got away. Frankly, the police don't have much to work with. I wouldn't worry if I were you."

"So I'm a *suspect?*"

"Relax. The guy had to file a complaint for his insurance. The police have other things to do."

Erich described the scene at his apartment and showed her photos on his cell phone. It seemed to him that, compared to earlier interviews, she wasn't taking many notes. Eventually she asked, "But it looks like nothing is missing? Is that right?"

"Far as I can tell." He felt a stab of pain in his temple. "Can't you do something for me?"

"We're working on it, Erich. But we won't clean up your mess. I already warned you to lie low for a while. Out by O'Hare there are plenty of cheap motels."

Erich drove home in a state of mounting rage. He didn't know if he'd call back the Denisons or seek out a motel, as she'd suggested. In any event, he needed a change of clothes. He needed to sort out a few affairs. Hell, Mrs. Kubek's grass needed cutting, but there wouldn't be time for that. He couldn't face putting his apartment in order. That task would have to wait for later.

When he parked his jeep at the curb, he was surprised to see a man in a suit jacket, wearing an earpiece, standing in front of his door. Obviously a cop.

"Mr. Ambrose! There you are. You've had a break in."

"I know that." At least Heffernan had sent somebody to the scene. "Do you have any good news for me?"

"In fact, we do."

Erich didn't feel inclined to invite him upstairs, so he accepted an invitation to talk in his car. He followed him to a blue sedan on the opposite side of the street. The fellow opened the door and Erich slid in, discovering a plump man in a yellow polo shirt. He offered his hand for Erich to shake.

"Hello. I'm Andre Plutov."

Oh Lord. Not the FBI!

Erich glanced the other way, wondering if he should bolt immediately. The man with the earpiece stood, arms folded, beside the door. He turned back to Plutov, who added, "May I have some of your time?"

His hand remained in the air, and now Erich shook it.

"We've been looking for you," Plutov said.

The Plan

HOUGH GRAY-HAIRED, his round cheeks gave him a cherubic, childish appearance. He had rosy skin and dark bristles coming out of his ears.

"What do you want?" Erich asked.

"It concerns my wife." He pronounced it *vife*. "Serena. She is..." He flapped a hand in front of his chest, as if searching for a word. "*Not* happy with you. You know that, I am sure."

Erich felt a thud in his stomach. "We've had a serious misunderstanding."

"So. Yes. That I see. Serena, she has been unhappy lately. But your misunderstanding can be seen as a common point between you. No? If you understand. Perhaps we can build on that. Take common point and make something constructive?"

Erich had no idea what the man was implying and he saw only one way to push back. "Listen," he said, "the law knows those men came from you. Same for the apartment. They're all over this situation. So you might as well stop now."

"Oh oh oh." Plutov shook his head. "*That* had nothing to do with me. You must believe. Not me. That was Serena. I did not know that she makes this big mistake until after. Friends tell me. Today I am here as a mediator. And maybe ask a little favor." He lifted his hands, joined his fingers.

A *favor*, Erich thought. This will not be good.

"Let us speak as one man to another." He leaned closer, not menacing but strangely friendly, as if he were trying to sell something. "Women insist on getting their way. Even when they should not have their way. What to do? You can fight. You can win. But it comes at a price." He smiled wearily. "Sometimes price is too high. You know what I mean, yes? You have a wife? You have a girlfriend?"

Erich didn't answer. Pictures of Alison were scattered on the floor of his apartment. It was like a wind had blown through his life and stirred up the past, images he'd tried very hard to file away.

Plutov seemed to interpret Erich's silence as assent.

"With women," he said, "we must be *smart*."

"Smart," Erich repeated.

"Yes, smart." Plutov tapped his forehead. "What happened to Viktor was most unfortunate but I believe it was an accident. It was not your intention. That I have been told."

Suddenly Erich pictured the Guatemalan nanny. She was the only other adult on the scene. Unlike Serena, she'd actually been in the room when Mr. Boots lost his cool. Yes, Plutov must've asked her about that day. She'd been his witness in defense. Erich felt a surge of gratitude, and now he was also certain that Plutov didn't know what had happened between Serena and him upstairs.

"Serena doesn't really want to hurt you," Plutov continued. "Please do not hold a grudge. She is not always herself. She has doctor and does better now. New prescription."

"She's been drunk whenever I've seen her," Erich said. "If you really want to be frank, that has to be said. It probably explains a lot of things. Especially if she's mixing it with meds."

Plutov cleared his throat. He gave a small roll of his shoulders which conceded the point but also suggested that he wasn't going to talk about this subject. It wasn't part of his pitch. "She has stopped drinking," Plutov affirmed. "She told me herself. Doctor's advice. She has resolved. This is good news."

Erich didn't believe him for an instant. He slid his fingers onto the door handle. Plutov continued, "Viktor was very troubled by this disagreeable rabbit of yours and when Viktor is troubled, his mother, she is upset, right? This is normal, right? Only she goes too far. She is what you call a drama queen, right? Especially with wrong prescription. But I am here to help you."

"Help me?"

"Yes, let us be frank. I cannot allow Serena to take foolish measures as she did against you. I have responsibilities and business and I cannot afford to be associated with such things. Listen: I am most serious. But Serena is a determined woman. Right? New prescription does not change everything, not for Viktor." He smiled ruefully. "This is the favor I ask. Serena and I have discussed you. I told her to leave it to me, I would take care of you."

Erich felt his head become very light. He wanted to flee but he had to hear what the man would say next.

"Here is the plan." He pointed his finger at Erich's chest. "No more talk with police, right? And no one touches you." He smiled. "I tell Serena you have been touched a little, and she believes me, she is happy. Especially since you will call her and say you are hurt. The ribs. You will beg her. That will convince her. You must tell what she wants to hear. Then it's over. Done. But you have not a scratch."

Plutov nodded, and Erich found himself nodding with him. "Not a scratch," Erich repeated. "I could do that."

"A few months from now," Plutov said, "everything forgotten. No harm done."

Erich couldn't bring himself to nod in agreement.

"Ah yes," Plutov added, "the rabbit. I hear that her boys did not find rabbit in your apartment. This is good for rabbit. I am glad. But still, we need a strategy about rabbit."

"Strategy?"

"Serena has ideas. She is a country girl. She wants to cook your rabbit for Viktor, for another party. To make her son happy. So we give her rabbit. That is not hard."

Plutov laughed. "Your face is a funny one. But no worry. I'm sure you like your magic rabbit. Your partner, right? He is safe. I won't touch him. Why go to so much trouble? I will get another rabbit, bring it to Serena, I say it is *your* rabbit. When you call Serena and tell her you are sore in ribs, you will also beg to get rabbit back. You plead, right? *'Please give me my rabbit!'* This makes her happy. She says *'No no no.'* You lose rabbit. And that is the end. She and Viktor make recipe with carrots. You safe and happy. Everyone happy!"

Slavoj Tupac

IT WAS A PLAN, wasn't it? If Andre Plutov could appease Serena and he could put this whole mess behind him with only a phone call, it seemed a no-brainer. Agent Heffernan had offered nothing remotely as efficient. He had little faith in her. What's more, his action wasn't breaking the law or helping somebody else to break the law. More likely, he was helping to put out a fire, in order to avoid further wrongdoing. They could turn the page. It would even make little Viktor happy, that snotnose.

The agreement was for Erich to wait till Monday night to call Serena. That would give Plutov time to set things up on his end. Rabbit procurement, and all the rest.

Erich enjoyed a calm weekend. You didn't fully appreciate the pleasures of domesticity, of luxuriating in your own snug corner, until it had been violently denied. Erich repaired his window and cleared the mess and used the occasion to sort out old clothes and throw out papers. He resisted the temptation to dawdle over Alison's photos; he reshelved and rearranged granddad Lou's books. Afterward, his place was tidy and Erich felt refreshed, as if he'd stepped out of sauna.

In preparation of his conversation with Serena Plutov, Erich practiced and tested different voices. This was the sort of task where Tom Denison excelled. From behind a curtain Tom could make you think you heard a feeble old man, or an excited boy with an Italian accent, or a woman doing the weather report on channel nine.

Erich pressed a hand to his throat. What was the right technique to play himself? A hoarse, desperate whisper? (*Unhhh*, he was clutching his sore ribs.) Or a high, panicky note? (*Ooooh*, he was forever chastened, repentant after a beating.) Erich laughed. He would be done with these people, once and for all.

On Monday morning he was sitting in Thurston's Diner, eating eggs and bacon with a big lump of feta cheese, when Agent Heffernan slid into the seat beside him. "Mornin'!" he said.

"Good morning, Erich."

This time, he wasn't annoyed to see her. If she wanted another face-to-face, this would save him a trip downtown. And the fact that she was back in his neighborhood suggested that she was taking his situation seriously, following up and doing her job.

"You're out early," he said. "Had breakfast?"

"Yes, thanks."

"They do blueberry pancakes here. Have you ever had the blueberry pancakes? Maybe you should try the blueberry pancakes."

"Stop it. No games, please. I'll come to the point. Do you have anything to tell me?"

Erich took a bite of toast and shook his head.

"Oh, fuck you. Come on!"

He stared. She'd never spoken to him like this before.

"What do you mean?"

"We know you met with Plutov on Saturday morning. Had a little talk in his car. You didn't call about that. Is he a friend of yours, Erich?"

"No!"

"What's that all about then? How long have you been in contact with him? Have you told him about your activities at Viktor's birthday party?"

"Hell no!"

"This is very unpleasant, Erich. This changes everything. Now I truly don't know whether I can trust you. Why believe *anything* you say? You held back information earlier and you were holding back just seconds ago. You pointedly avoided mentioning him. How many times have you spoken to Andre Plutov?"

"That was the first time, I swear. I didn't go looking for him. He came for me."

"And what's he want from you?"

Erich told her the truth, and tried to make her see that he'd done nothing in bad faith. He put it all down to the story of Mr. Boots. "See, Serena wasn't joking when she threatened me about the rabbit. I'd thought that part was just winding me up, and this weird bullshit was her way to go about it. But no. She actually means it! She's mental, I'm telling you. That's what Plutov wanted to talk to me about."

The waitress came by and Agent Heffernan ordered a coffee. Then she shrugged. "I don't know, Erich. Even if I could believe you, you don't seem to grasp the gravity of the situation. Plutov has former connections with the FSB. Lots of those guys came straight out of the KGB. He has more than a few rabbits in his closet, if you catch my drift. How do you think somebody like

Serena had access to hired hands? These aren't the kind of people she meets at her squash club in Wilmette. And now you tell me they'll turn around and play nice with you?"

"I hear you. But maybe you're too distracted by Plutov, when it's really Serena that you ought to worry about. She's the one. She—" Erich groped for a way to make Agent Heffernan see. To grasp the nature of the threat. *She was trained in 4-H. A homecoming queen gone off the rails.* He repeated his story, one more time.

"I'll get back to you," she said. "Or I won't." Then she stood up and walked out the door, leaving Erich with the check for her coffee.

After breakfast, Erich went to work at Wendall's Original Organics, showing up earlier than usual. He saw Staci in front of her garage with a tall young man in black capri shorts. His silver tank-top revealed finely muscled arms. "Hi!" Erich called, drawing nearer.

Staci's cell phone rang. "I have to take this. Erich, could you tell Slavoj about the rotation sequence?"

The young man smiled at Erich. "Hello. Nice to meet you. Call me Tupac, if you like."

"Tupac?"

"People stumble on Slavoj, though Staci pronounces it very well, I must say. It's Slovene. I've written about Tupac, so it's sort of a nickname, you see. Everyone knows Tupac."

The fellow's English was very good, only slightly accented. "Whatever you like," Erich said, avoiding either name. "Come over here." He took him to the dry storage area and pointed out the drainage racks, the recessed fittings. The system was simple but very effective. He showed him how to prep and stack the trays. "So," Erich said, "first visit to Chicago?"

"Oh, not a visit. I live here. I'm a graduate student at Northwestern."

"That so? What's your area?"

"Post-structuralist sustainability. Mainly I work on biotexts."

Erich shrugged. "Well, that's what we grow here."

Slavoj nodded, and Erich wondered: Did I just say something smart?

Erich led him through the main growing space, demonstrated the track lights, and answered Slavoj's questions. Staci called from the door. "Erich, could you come here for a minute?"

He left Slavoj pondering a shelf of micro-greens and followed her across the driveway. Staci looked flushed, a bit stressed, and Erich wondered if her phone call had brought bad news. But, a moment later, when she pulled a wad of twenties out of her pocket, he had an inkling of the reason.

"I'm truly sorry about this. But I want to do what's best for everyone, from a systemic perspective, while at the same time following the wisdom of my heart. And this is what I've decided. It's just not working out, Erich. We don't have the same vision. I'm not assigning blame here, that's not the point. Let's move past that narrative, shall we? The point is: I've decided to go with Slavoj."

"You're saying I'm fired? He's replacing me?"

"I owe you for last week and the time and trouble it took you to come today." She sat on a bricked ledge bordering the driveway, next to a bed of marigolds, and began counting out bills. "Twenty—forty—sixty—" He watched, noticing that when she reached a desired figure, she hesitated, before adding one more bill. A little stroke for her conscience?

"You're saying I'm fired?" he repeated.

Perverse, but he wanted to hear the word. It wasn't only money that she owed him. He was dealing with the FBI and the Russians and a violent nutjob, and the least she could do, as a courtesy, was to say the word.

"You know our history, Erich. This was always just a job for you." She held out the cash, and he took it.

"I don't see what's wrong with that."

Slavoj stepped out to the driveway. "Where do I—?" He saw that they were deep in discussion and he hastened back to the garage.

"Right," Staci said. "You don't see what's wrong, do you? Exactly. We understand each other. We all make our life choices.

"For fuck's sake, Staci. You sell salad."

"And what do you do?" She walked away.

The Call

"SERENA? SERENA? *Serena?*" There, that was it. A lower pitch. That was the tone he'd use for his call. Bruised. Contrite. He took a deep breath and punched out her number.

She answered after two rings. "Hello?"

"*Serena?*" He swallowed. "Hi, this is Erich." He swallowed again. "You know, Ambrose?"

"What do you want?"

"I'm just calling to say: enough! Okay? I've learned my lesson. I want out of this. You've got my rabbit. We're even now, right?"

"You don't say?"

"I can't take anymore," he croaked. "Please..."

There was a silence.

"You are so full of shit, do you know that?"

"What?"

"That wasn't the same rabbit. Viktor said your rabbit had colored feet. You think my son is stupid? You don't fool anybody, magic man. You think I can't see when my husband is lying? What a crock! You guys are so lame."

Erich paced across his kitchen linoleum, for a moment at a loss for words. Eventually he blurted: "I don't know what you're talking about."

"Oh my. Tell you what, Ambrose. I've got an opening in my schedule tomorrow afternoon. Come by the house around three o'clock. You know where to find me. Bring your bunny. Do that or you'll be sorry."

Serena hung up.

Paging Mr. Boots

WHEN ERICH WAS TWELVE years old, he'd received a wrist guillotine for Christmas. It was great fun. Solid oak and thirty inches high, with a stainless steel blade, it had two holes at the bottom. You could stick your wrist in the upper hole. In the hole directly beneath it, you could place a piece of fruit, an apple or an orange. Then you slammed down the blade! The fruit was chopped in half. Miraculously, however, your wrist remained intact, despite the appearance of the blade passing through it. Yes, a fun trick!

Not cheap, though. Erich received such a fancy Christmas present because, a month earlier, his birthday present had been a flop. He'd torn away the wrapping paper and found a box containing the unassembled pieces of a replica paddle boat designed by Leonardo da Vinci. It was an educational toy, one of da Vinci's original inventions that combined technical ingenuity and subtle aesthetic sense, based on the shapes and movements of fish.

"What is it?"

His parents explained, and Erich struggled not to throw down the box and stamp away from the table. How could they be so stupid?

"Oh," he said, his throat tightening. "Thank you."

They could see his disappointment, and they tried to reassure him. "You can put it on a shelf in your room when it's finished," his mother told him. His father opened the box and slid out the sectioned contents. "Here, Erich. I'll help you."

It was a project that lasted weeks, putting together that miserable boat. His father did most of the work, but Erich dutifully helped him. Once his father broke a paddle piece and swore terribly. Gluing it together was painstaking. When the boat was finally finished, his father's relief was as great as his own. "Isn't it pretty?" his mother said, when they put it on the shelf. Not once did any of them admit aloud what was really happening, that they only pretended that all was cheery and chipper among themselves. It seemed to be the modus operandi of the household. "Nice boat," they agreed.

But his parents made it up to him on Christmas. The wrist guillotine was terrific. *Slam!* There went another orange. Erich laughed.

"Slow down!" his mother said. "We're not going to waste fruit."

"Hey Dad!" Erich called. "The instructions say you can do a version with a fake hand, so it looks like your hand falls off! Wouldn't that be cool? It's in your magic catalogue. I want to get one of those fake hands."

"You'll have to save up for it."

That was origin of Erich's first attempts to put together his own magic act, before his later embrace of close up performance. He had a childish fascination for gore, tricks involving needles and blades and fake blood, a contrasting sensibility with his parents' adult act, their emphasis on dance and shiny silks and doves. He acquired a collection of fake hands and remembered selling them a few years later to a twelve-year old going through a similar stage. He thanked the kid and then went out and spent the money on a case of beer.

Viktor Plutov was nine years old. That's what Erich remembered from the birthday cake. That was a bit young for the bloodthirsty stage, wasn't it? Especially if it weren't a trick but some version of the real thing. Did the kid really want to skin a rabbit, or was he just being egged on by his screwy mom? Not nice to think about. All was not cheery and chipper among the Plutovs. That much was certain.

Still, regarding Mr. Boots, Erich picked up the phone and called Greg Griffin, just to test the waters. He hadn't made up his mind, but he wanted to know his options.

"Hey Greg, looks like I got another gig for a kid show. Hoping you can help me out."

"Really? Another one? Who for?"

Greg's tone was suspicious, typically unprofessional. His clients were none of Greg's business. Still, to appease him, Erich invented a story on the spot: "A guy name Wilson in Sheboygan. Twin girls, party by the water. Picnic. I won't need to rent any equipment, just a rabbit. Say, tell you what, man. I'll buy him off you. Name your price. Same rabbit as the last show."

"You're going all the way to Sheboygan?" Greg was curious. "Gee. That's like one hundred and fifty miles."

"Is that so?" Erich replied.

"They must be paying you well."

Erich sighed. "Respectable. Good enough. So, what do you say? How much for Mr. Boots?"

"You want Mr. Boots?"

Erich slashed the air with his fist, several times, trying to keep his voice neutral. "I'm pretty sure that was the rabbit I used last time. I suspect you remember it, too. Don't you, Greg?"

A silence.

"Gee, I don't know, Erich."

"What's your price? Give me a number."

"Since that day, he hasn't been the same. I don't know what happened. But Mr. Boots is no longer his old self."

"I'll take my chances. Come on, Greg! You got other rabbits. You can spare this one."

"When's your show?"

Now Erich exploded. "What the fuck difference does it make? What's it to you? Can't you just be normal?"

"Hold on there. I don't like that, not one bit." Greg was offended. "I don't just hand over my rabbits to anyone."

The conversation ended without a deal. Greg had a moral investment in his rabbits. It was frustrating, though Erich couldn't deny that what he had in mind for Mr. Boots was not a happy fate.

Erich turned on his computer. "Well, there are more fish in the sea!" He typed out a word search and brought up a list of pet shops. "There are plenty of rabbits. . .in the sea!"

He scrolled through the possibilities. A white rabbit with charcoal feet. It couldn't be that hard.

But the first couple of places he called told him a different story. "No, sorry, can't help you there." And: "No, we don't have one like that. Actually, I've worked here eight years and we've gone through a lot of rabbits and I don't think I've ever seen one like that. But listen, we got some new gray angoras, just beautiful, lop-eared, you'd be very happy with a—"

"No thanks!" Erich hung up.

There were other numbers to call, but as he looked over the list, another plan came to mind. This search was taking up too much time. Why not keep it simple?

That night, he parked his jeep a block away from Greg's house and walked the rest of the distance, cutting through a neighbor's back yard. Crickets creaked, and a lawn sprinkler went *spitch, spitch, spitch.*

Erich bent over the rabbit hutch.

"Come on now," he whispered. "Come on, little buddy."

A scuffling as Boots slipped past his hand and squeezed into a corner of the cage. Erich leaned in, stretched as far as he could reach. Easy. . .easy. . .he grabbed him by the scruff, and then lifted him out. Boots' hind feet paddled the air.

"Here we go."

Erich dropped him in a pillow case. He bunched up the top and slung it over his shoulder.

He slipped quietly out of the back yard, keeping under the shadows of trees, chuckling to himself.

The Blessing

HAT NIGHT, HE PUT MR. BOOTS to bed in his bathtub and brought him some of Staci's organic microgreens, which the rabbit began to mow down furiously. "You get the fancy stuff for your last meal," Erich said. "Enjoy."

He covered the tub with an old window-screen from the kitchen so the rabbit couldn't jump out. Before retiring, Erich checked his cell phone. He'd turned it off during his furtive visit to Greg Griffin's back yard. Now he discovered a voicemail from Agent Heffernan.

"I want to stress, Erich, that you should keep your distance from the Plutovs. You really don't want to go there. You've been warned."

That was it. No goodbye, no further explanation. Erich listened to the voicemail three times.

Lying in bed, Erich fidgeted with his sheet. Was Agent Heffernan threatening him? Or giving him a heads up? Her people had been monitoring the Plutovs, and she had access to information that he couldn't know. But he couldn't bring himself to feel grateful. Heffernan offered no concrete help. No assurance about his situation. Her input was all negative. *You don't want to go there.* Was that general advice, regarding any transaction, or did she mean it literally: he should stay away from the house?

He was unable to sleep and various scenarios played out in his mind. Maybe he was a sucker to hope that tomorrow he could hand over Mr. Boots and all would be well. Maybe he'd ring the bell in Wilmette and the door would open to an angry man with broken fingers, gripping a baseball bat in his good hand. *"Sweetheart!"*

He got up to use the bathroom. On the other hand, he thought, Agent Heffernan's word didn't mean much, whereas Serena's desire for this rabbit had been confirmed. He looked over at Mr. Boots, a shadow behind the screen. "Sorry, dude. It's gonna be you."

It took him a long time to fall asleep, and the next morning he awoke after a confused dream of Alison standing shirtless and talking matter-of-factly about fish. It didn't make any sense but she was *there*. It had been a while since he'd had one of those dreams. He stepped out of the bedroom, her voice still in his ears, to discover Mr. Boots chewing on the living room rug.

He'd managed to knock aside the window-screen and escape the tub. The damage to the rug was impressive: a large bald patch, bordered by a ragged welter of threads. Mr. Boots grabbed a thread and pulled it back, chewing meditatively, like a connoisseur in a taste test. Erich clapped his hands. "Stop!" The rabbit let go and seized another thread, ripping it out, chewing. He was very methodical; maybe it was therapeutic for him. When Erich came closer, he ran under the coffee table and then around to the other end of the couch. He was a crafty little fucker.

Erich went to the kitchen and put on the coffee pot. He opened his laptop and checked his email, trying to clear his mind and form a plan, all the while thinking of granddad Lou's advice: *leave the room*. He considered his options. He wasn't broke—living rent-free for a year had left him with some savings. Where should he go? He'd always wanted to visit Canada.

His phone rang, but the caller I.D. indicated Greg Griffin, so he didn't answer. A short time later his phone beeped to indicate a new voicemail. Then it beeped again with a text message from Greg: CALL ME.

He turned back to his laptop and typed a search for Alison Keating. This time of year she and the Perfesser were at their summer camp. In a few clicks, he found the website for "Embrace Your Aesthetic." He saw Alison's photo, a publicity still dating back to when they were still married. Her high cheekbones, her gaze toward a spot off-camera. He remembered the day she'd brought home an envelope of samples and he'd helped her choose this shot. "*That* one," he'd said. "Very pretty!" By now she'd had the baby. According to the website, she'd taught Beginning Acting last week. This week she was teaching a course on mime.

Let it go, he thought. You have to let it go.

That's what Fred told him. And he'd tried, he'd really tried. But maybe the "it" wasn't his life with Alison but rather the rut and bad habits he'd embraced, which he could continue to put behind him, without abandoning *her*. Wasn't that a possible distinction? The idea had haunted him for a long time and in the current circumstances the truth of this insight pressed itself home. The past was past, the present was entangled, but the future was still unformed, full of possibility. He had to embrace that potential! He took nothing for granted and didn't expect miracles but he needed to see Alison, and tell her, to let her know how much he'd changed. The situation could evolve. The rest was just noise. He should listen to his own heart, not to Serena or Agent Heffernan. He could leave Chicago—hell, that part was easy.

He packed a suitcase and a duffle bag, and gathered a few important papers, a couple of granddad Lou's books. On a whim he took his dumbbells. There was room in the jeep. He found Bonnie Kubek's key and let himself in her back door, calling softly, "It's only me, Bonnie." He descended to the basement where amid canning jars he spied Spud's old travel cage. He'd seen her use it when she took Spud to the vet, or when she visited her sister in Waukesha.

He dusted it off. Plenty big for a rabbit!

It took a couple of minutes to corral Mr. Boots, and to vacuum up his shit pellets. But soon Erich was rolling along in the jeep, the travel cage in the front seat next to him. He said to the cage, "You caught a break, brother. You're gonna meet your Uncle Fred."

He couldn't leave town without telling Fred, and asking his blessing. Besides, a rabbit could keep Fred company, cheer up his place. He parked on Auburn Avenue, a neighborhood of tilting streetlamps and potholes. Fred's building was surrounded by beaten grass, littered with energy drink cans. There was no intercom or buzzer; he carried the cage up two flights of stairs and banged on Fred's door.

"YAH?"

Before Erich could answer, it opened to a lean man with a wispy beard. He coughed into his fist and stared.

"Who is it, Manny?" came Fred's voice.

"I'm Erich," Erich said. "Fred knows me."

"Erich!" Fred called. "Come on in!"

Manny stepped aside and Erich entered the room, where Fred sat on a straight-backed chair, his head tilted back, with rolled up pieces of toilet paper stuffed in his nostrils.

"We got ourselves a situation here," said Fred.

Erich put down the cage. "Jesus, what happened?"

Fred laughed. "Oh, it's not too bad. My blood pressure, you know, it goes wacky on me and sometimes my vessels burst and a nosebleed can be the worst. Son of a bitch just doesn't stop! I'm like a faucet. It got away from me last week in Walgreens and they found me on the floor and when I woke up, the medics said I almost died, can you believe that? After some of the shit

I pulled off in my day, I die of a nosebleed?" Fred laughed again, his feet shuffling on the floor.

As usual, the TV was blaring, and now a gameshow audience clapped enthusiastically.

"Mind if I turn that down a bit?" Erich asked.

"Suit yourself."

"I'll see you later," said the wispy-bearded man.

He slipped out the door, and Fred called, "Don't forget what we talked about!"

Erich put down the remote control, grabbed a chair and scooted up next to Fred. "So, how are you doing, man? It's been a while."

"Good. Good. Was gonna ask you the same question."

"Ups and downs," Erich said. "I've been sober though, I can say that much."

Fred grinned his snaggle teeth. With the toilet paper in his nostrils, he reminded Erich of a walrus. "Well there you go. You're still in the ball game."

It was an expression Fred often used. To be sober was to be in the ball game. The score might be good or it might be bad, but even if it were the latter, a positive result was not beyond your grasp, because it wasn't over yet, you were in the game. Just staying in was a kind of success. On the other hand, if you weren't sober, you were on the bench, watching. The game could feel unbearably long, from that position. You started looking for ways to end it.

"Who was that guy?" Erich asked.

"Oh, that's Manny. I'm letting him stay here for a while."

There were wads of clothes on either side of Fred's narrow bed; it was impossible to tell what might belong to Fred or to someone else. But, in any case, there wasn't much room for Mr. Boots.

"The kid's in a bad way," Fred said. "Nowhere else to go. Heroin is terrible stuff." He shook his head, and then reached up and adjusted a tissue in his nostril with a little corking twist. "He has to decide for himself. Has to hit bottom." He fine-tuned the other nostril. "I'm afraid Manny's not there yet."

The observation was grim, but Fred's manner also suggested that hitting bottom was something to look forward to, because then Manny could hope to get better.

"I'm going on a trip," Erich announced. "Wanted to stop by before I went."

Fred's eyeballs screwed to one side, taking in the cage. "Interesting luggage."

"My jeep's parked in the sun so I brought it inside." There was a pause, and Erich decided not to ask Fred this favor.

"How long you gonna be away?"

"I'm not sure, Fred. I don't know."

"Uh huh." Fred's jaw tensed, and he added, "How much trouble you in?"

"I wouldn't put it that way. This trip is exploratory. That's how I think of it."

"Life's a freakin' adventure. Well, good luck to you." And then, Fred changed the subject. He must've sensed that Erich didn't want to justify himself, and he accepted the fact. "So, you gonna show me a trick?"

From anyone else, this question was an unwelcome cliché. Strangers often said this when they learned that Erich was a magician, though they wouldn't dream of asking for a spontaneous performance from a person in another line of work, say a singer or a doctor. ("Let's hear a song!" or "Feel my prostate!") For some reason, magicians were expected to work for free, at the snap of somebody else's fingers.

But it was different with Fred. When he said it, Erich didn't mind. He reached in his pocket and pulled out a twenty dollar bill. He rolled it up into a firm cylinder, like a tooter. Then he executed a clean move and made it vanish.

"Nice!" Fred laughed.

Now Erich performed the recovery, extracting the bill from Fred's front shirt pocket.

"You got me again," Fred said.

These moves were old school cigarette manipulation, straight out of granddad Lou's act. There wasn't much call for cigarette tricks nowadays. But rolled bills could serve as a substitute. After displaying the twenty, Erich slid it back into Fred's front shirt pocket. "How you doing for money, Fred?"

"I'm okay."

Suddenly Fred stood up and moved unsteadily to the door, his head tilted back with the wadded tissues in his nostrils. He opened the door, inspected the landing, and then closed it again. He wobbled back to his chair.

"What's the matter?" Erich asked, helping him to sit down.

"I thought Manny might be listening. He's very resourceful, you know. Some things he doesn't need to hear."

"Uh huh."

"I just get dizzy sometimes. It'll go away."

"I can take you to a doctor, Fred."

"Drop it, man."

Erich gave him two hundred dollars, which Fred instructed him to hide in two different places in his room. "You sure?" Erich asked. "I don't like this Manny."

"No, it's okay, I got it under control. We have an understanding. I don't let him shoot up or turn tricks in the room. It's gonna be fine."

They chatted a little longer, and then Erich said his goodbye. As he walked out the door, Fred gripped the sides of his chair and called, "Hang tough. Stay in the game. And don't forget, I got your back!"

CHARLES HOLDEFER

CALL OF THE NORTH

Inhabit the Being

FTER SEEING FRED, he visited the main branch of his bank. Regulations didn't allow him to liquidate his account completely, but he walked out of the lobby with $4000 stuffed in his pocket. He'd never carried such a wad of cash, but he didn't want to rely on his credit card, which was traceable. From the bank he drove straight to the I-94 ramp, northbound. In less than an hour he'd crossed the border into Wisconsin.

Erich had good memories of Wisconsin. When he was a child, his parents often took "A Touch of Ambrosia" up north. Erich had sat in the back seat of the car, nestled among equipment and a cage of doves, while his father's airy blond afro blocked his view of the windshield. In summer, Wisconsin meant cool lakes and piney scents, sweet corn and walleye and bratwurst in towns with German names on storefronts. String cheese! He recalled visiting the Houdini Museum in Appleton, inspecting the posters and props of his namesake: handcuffs, iron leg shackles, straightjackets from Houdini's escape act. Fearsome-looking stuff.

Winter in Wisconsin was a roaring fire at a stony hearth beneath the mounted head of a buck deer, with friendly, fat strangers calling to him while he waited in the lobby for his parents to start their show: "Hey little buddy, come on back to the kitchen! You like prime rib?" That was the supper club circuit. Those gigs no longer existed, in an era of Internet and a hundred other forms of entertainment. Those days were as irretrievable as the Bronze Age. Still, as Erich surveyed the map, he felt a happy pinch of nostalgia at the names of certain towns. He was sure that "A Touch of Ambrosia" had performed in Wauwatosa and Packwaukee.

He spent the night in a town called Lee Point Landing, in a musty motel room with burgundy wallpaper and a sign in the bathroom warning *DO NOT CLEAN FISH*. Early the next morning he was awakened by another call from Greg Griffin, which he didn't pick up. He deleted his messages and switched his phone off.

For breakfast he ate waffles at a truck stop and, further down the road, he pulled over and ripped dandelion greens out of a ditch and brought them to Mr. Boots. He pondered how he would proceed. Alison and the Perfesser had their "Embrace Your Aesthetic" camp near Lake Muskalooga. That was about two hours to the northwest. He couldn't presume that she could take time off to see him. These camps kept her very busy. He would have to make his presence legitimate. She was the person who understood him better than anyone in the world. Whatever it took, he would try.

The road to Lake Muskalooga was a narrow blacktop winding past dairy farms. Eventually he saw signs for boat rentals and fish bait, and then, an arrow: *Embrace Your Aesthetic, 2 miles.* "It's show time!" he told Mr. Boots.

The young man at the reception was snippy. "Sir, the course started two days ago. You haven't registered online? You're a walk-in?" He assumed an air of put-upon authority, though clearly he was just a college theater major with a summer job. At first everything seemed impossible, but Erich made it clear that he would pay the full fee. He filled out a form, checking the box for a private cabin, hesitating at the line where he was supposed to write his name. He marked "Eric Boots."

The young man invited him to swipe his card, and Eric replied, "Cash okay?" He didn't wait for an answer but counted out bills as the kid looked on, frowning.

He gathered up his registration packet which included an "Embrace Your Aesthetic" T-shirt and he went back to the jeep to retrieve his suitcase and Mr. Boots. It required several trips down a bumpy foot trail of cedar chips to move into his cabin. Pine trees gave way to hardwoods and ferns; the air was muggy and gnats buzzed in his face. A web of trails encircled the camp complex which offered a community center, a cafeteria, an outdoor amphitheater and a chapel, beside the lake and a boat launch.

The cabin was Spartan. Just a mattress on sagging springs, a wooden desk and a straight-backed chair. The young man at the reception had promised to send up some bedding. Toilets and showers were available further up the trail.

Erich dragged his chair across the plank floor and set it outside where he would have more air. He read the brochure about the course, entitled *Inhabit the Being of Mime*. A packed schedule of lectures and workshops, leading up to dress rehearsals and a final gala performance on Saturday night. When not in class or engaged in craft discussions, participants were encouraged to "inhabit the being." Instead of speaking, they should communicate nonverbally, using a body vocabulary to develop their own "personal idiolect of gesture" which would distinguish them as individual artists.

Geez, Erich thought. Alison sounds very serious about this stuff. This camp is no fooling around.

Her true love was acting and musical theater, he knew, but like many of her peers, she'd dabbled in dance and mime. The Perfesser had written articles on those subjects, and in recent years, there had been a mime revival: the market was overcrowded with traditional acting classes and competition to attract paying students was ferocious. With mime, Erich suspected, the Perfesser had found his niche. His cash cow.

Erich slipped on his blue "Embrace Your Aesthetic" T-shirt. The brochure advised participants to wear their shirts to all group sessions. He hurried down the cedar chip path, checking his watch. He would be in time for lunch.

He heard the cafeteria before he saw it—laughter and cries, children's voices. Emerging from the trees, he discovered a log structure with open windows. On one side, children enjoyed a raucous meal, shouting and pounding their tables. They wore yellow shirts. According to the brochure, they were here for a camp to learn about puppet theater. On the other side, a smaller group of adults in blue shirts sat at a long table, not speaking but gesturing and nodding among themselves.

Erich entered and approached the adults. "Excuse me. May I join you?"

A man smiled. He didn't answer but he stood and made a circular motion in front of his stomach, and then pointed to a salad bar and stack of trays.

So Erich endured his first silent meal. He didn't manage to communicate beyond an occasional nod or shrug while other people swayed or gesticulated, employing much wrist action. He'd barely finished eating when everyone stood up, and he followed them to the community center, where the afternoon seminar would take place.

As soon as they crossed the threshold, the atmosphere changed. People chatted with aggressive cheerfulness, expending their pent-up energies. "Hi! Hi! Who are you? What's your name? Where you from?"

Erich answered their questions and took a chair in the circle. They already knew each other, this much was obvious. A smiling, chipmunky fellow introduced himself as Ron and announced that Erich should get ready for a *special* time. "We've got a super teacher. You'll like her."

"She's very dynamic!" piped a lady with a sunburned nose.

"Everybody gets to share."

"Sometimes we start a little late, though," volunteered another. "She's nursing a baby."

When Alison made her entrance, she mimed surprise, reeling from her shoulders, as if she hadn't expected to see the group, and everyone laughed. "Okay!" she said, "today we start with open format Q & A. Anything that you're wondering about after your first days of Inhabitation, now's the time to ask." She looked at a piece of paper in her hand. "But a quick question. Eric Boots? Is there—"

Now she noticed Erich, who'd been out of her direct line of vision. She fell silent, her lips pressed tightly together, and then she recovered herself to say to the group, "We have a new member."

"Hello," Erich said. "Sorry to arrive late for the course, but I've cleared it with the reception." He gave a little nod. "Glad to be here."

Alison crinkled the piece of paper between her fingers. "Nice to see you. Could you step out with me for a moment? I'd like to bring you up to speed on a few things you missed." Then she addressed the group. "Will you excuse us?"

People appeared surprised as Erich followed her out the door. She pounded down the steps and went to a picnic table under a tree, far enough away so that they wouldn't be heard through the window.

"What the hell, Erich! What kind of stunt is this?"

"I needed to see you."

"*Here?* In my course?"

"I know you're busy and I'll respect the structure. I'm not going to cause any trouble. I'll fit in."

"You, mime? Give me a break."

"There's—"

"Don't want to hear it. Nope. I've got people waiting. They paid for this time. Here's the deal: I cannot accept any disruption. You might weasel your way in but I can show your ass out. Through the front door. Understand? Now, I've got work to do. If you want to talk to me, it'll have to be later."

"Fine," he said. "I hear you."

He hadn't expected her to be so flustered but when they returned to the community center, as if with a magical snap of the fingers, Alison was instantly composed and pleasant. He had to give her credit—she was all business and carried it off like a pro. "Let's jump right in, shall we?" It felt strange yet utterly familiar to be in the same room with her again, to hear her voice, to let his eyes linger on her, to notice that little sweeping gesture with her left hand when she made a point. (That was very Alisonesque.) A nostalgic charge coursed through Erich. I love you I love you I love you.

There were changes, too. Her breasts—he'd never seen them like *that*. Wow. He made a concentrated effort not to stare too openly. He shouldn't make her uncomfortable. Trying to keep his face neutral, Erich was sure that he did a better job at not staring than the fellow called Ron on the other side of the circle. Ron was rapt, ogling Alison like an infatuated third-grader.

"I want to hear more about your inhabitation," she told them. "You've had a couple of days to work on it. Do you feel your body vocabulary is growing?"

People nodded and agreed that the exercises of previous workshops had proved very useful. "Before, when I did the invisible wall, I relied too much on my hands, you know?" said a young woman in goth gear, with one half of her head shaved. Her name was Polly. "Now I'm getting both shoulders and upper neck into it. It's great!"

There was a spontaneous murmur of assent, as participants moved their arms, touching invisible walls in the air, experimenting with angles of grip. One man, though, shook his head and insisted that a lower center of gravity was necessary: you couldn't properly perform an invisible wall without action from the hips. He sprang up. "Let me show you."

For over a minute he labored in the center of the circle, sometimes grunting against space. Erich had the impression that he wasn't the only one whose attention strayed during this demonstration. Alison gently reminded, "Our focus today is discussion, not performance." Finally he sat down.

"One thing I'm struggling with as a mime," said a man, his eyes darting from side to side, "and I'll just come out and say it, all right? Put it out there. Is. . .is it okay to be fat?"

Of course it was! Everyone agreed, and expressed a common purpose, a shared solidarity with the Silent Invisible. One young fellow in low-slung jeans confided, "Don't let it bug you. It's like the old joke, 'nobody wants to fuck a mime.' But I can tell you, it's not true."

A few people frowned, and an older man's hand shot up. "Yes, Larry?" said Alison. "Go ahead."

"Listen, I'm no prude," said Larry. "When I was in the navy I heard the f-bomb all day long. But is that kind of talk necessary here? I'm using mime in my youth ministry and that's exactly the kind of attitude I want to discourage. I mean no offense."

A woman beside him nodded, and the young man replied, "Well, I meant no offense either. It's just. . ." He slouched, made a helpless gesture. He wasn't going to back down, but then Alison interjected, "words words words!" She feigned tightening a rope around her neck. "Aren't we glad we're learning mime?"

Everyone laughed, and a confrontation was avoided. They spoke of warm-up techniques, and tips for sustaining concentration, to remain in the moment of inhabitation. Then they did pair work, taking turns helping each other with "walking against the wind" and "leaning on an invisible table." It was quickly apparent that the skill level of the participants was varied. Pastor Larry and his lady-friend were quite good; so was goth Polly. Erich felt clumsy but when he saw one middle-aged man gesticulate and lurch around the room like a bear swatting bees, he took comfort that he wasn't the worst person in the group. Working with Ron was a different kind of trial: his "Embrace Your Aesthetic" T-shirt reeked of sweat. It was unpleasant to stand close to him.

At the end of the session, Alison passed out photocopies with tomorrow's assignment. People filed out the door, and several classmates scuttled straight to Alison, clinging and asking more questions. Erich saw it wasn't a good time to talk. He shouldn't appear pressing. He went back to his cabin where he found a bundle of bedding in a plastic bag beside his door. He went inside and made up his bed, and removed Mr. Boots from his cage and cleaned it. Rather than try to catch the rabbit again, Erich let him run free in the cabin and lay back on his mattress to peruse his assignment, entitled "Telling a Story." It wasn't enough, apparently, to grapple with the Silent Invisible. You were supposed to make sense of it.

Mr. Boots acted timid at first, but soon he thumped around the floorboards as if he owned the place. Erich fetched him more greens, and improvised a water dish. When he left the cabin to go to dinner, he didn't bother to recapture Mr. Boots but he carefully closed the door behind him.

At the evening meal, Erich struck up the acquaintance a few classmates: the fat man, named Evan, taught high school biology in a Milwaukee suburb; Polly was from the Twin Cities, a statistics major at the University of Minnesota. Other mimes were uninterested in a new arrival and conversed among themselves, while a hardcore group didn't speak at all, but maintained the Inhabitation Protocol that Erich had witnessed at lunch. They communicated only by gesture and facial expression. This wasn't part of the official program, but a schism in the group was emerging, it seemed, between dinner-talkers and zealots. There was also some serious flirting going on between Polly and the young fellow in slow-slung jeans. Erich felt a stab at the memory that Alison and the Perfesser had met in a theater workshop. The proximity, the imperative to show oneself and share, slid easily into a sexual vibe.

After the meal, the evening agenda offered a screening of a Chaplin film, but Erich decided to go back to his cabin, where he found Mr. Boots chewing on the leg of his desk. It was dry, crumbly wood, and there was a considerable pile of splinters on the floor. The rabbit looked happily occupied, so Erich decided to leave him to his demolition. He pulled off his clothes, switched off the light and lay back on the mattress. He was tired from driving and from the emotions of the day. Serena Plutov and the sound of her laughter seemed far, far away. He wanted to rehearse what he would say to Alison, the right way to unburden his heart and affirm his love. But words eluded him and were replaced by fresh images of Alison, her gestures, her expressive face, which made him aware of distances he had yet to travel, a frustrating persistence of invisible walls.

The Perfesser

THE NEXT MORNING, the discussion in Alison's class took a political turn. A young man named T.J. who hadn't said much the previous day raised his hand. "I have a question about the show on Saturday night when we tell our story? Right. I was reading in the brochure that we're supposed to wear full costume and make-up? Now, I don't see why anybody should have to wear whiteface. You can take the art seriously without those outdated conventions. It's like a kind of reverse minstrel show. It's creepy and I don't like it."

T.J. was one of the few African-Americans in the group. There were only two. (Or was it three? In the seconds that followed T.J.'s remark, Erich's thoughts made a hasty inventory: it was hard to say about the pastor's lady-friend, Bette. Were other people wondering the same thing? Should they be thinking about this difference at all? Or was it disrespectful to ignore it? What did this all mean?) Alison nodded after T.J. spoke, but she didn't immediately respond.

Polly said, "Isn't it just a mask to make everybody neutral? I don't see it as being about race."

"So when people used blackface it wasn't about race?"

"That was different, of course."

"So things are racial when it's black but not when it's white. White is normative?"

"Nobody said that," said a gray-haired woman unhappily clutching a paper coffee cup.

Now Alison spoke: "Why don't we foreground and problematize the issue by using, say, green? That could be interesting."

"Oh sure," said Evan. "I've always wanted to be Kermit the Frog."

Some people laughed, some people frowned. Was Evan trivializing a serious question? For the first time, Alison appeared rattled. But the discussion was interrupted by a knock on the door. "Yes? Come in."

The snippy young man from the reception cabin entered, his flip-flops slapping with every step. "Got another one for you." He looked down at his card. "This is Doug."

"Hi Doug!" everyone called.

The new student didn't reply but instead acknowledged the greeting by lifting his fingertips to his chin, suddenly sweeping them upward and outward, miming an enormous smile. Several classmates mimed their own smiles in return, or put a hand over their heart and fluttered. It occurred to Erich to insert a finger in his throat as if to vomit, but he didn't bother.

Alison devoted a few minutes of class time to explain to Doug about the group and the plans for the gala show. Everyone else listened patiently, observing Doug's golf shorts and boating shoes. (Was he successful and gay, or just one or the other? Hmmm.) Alison emphasized the *good working atmosphere* that was so essential to collaborative arts and to this class in particular. This felt like an allusion to the earlier argument about color, though she ventured nothing more specific. The rest of the morning was devoted to critiquing performance sequences that individuals were trying to integrate into a narrative, to tell their story. The same man as yesterday—Erich could never quite get his name straight—sprang up and went to the center of the circle and began to press on his invisible wall. "Watch my hips," he reminded them.

When they finally stopped for lunch, Erich hoped to pull Alison aside and speak for at least a few minutes. He'd spent more time in her presence in the last twenty-four hours than he had in the previous year, but they'd exchanged only a few words. Her proximity gave him a buzz.

But, like the previous day, people converged on Alison at the end of class. Ron thrust himself at her, and as soon as she paused to listen, others arrived, forming a small circle. Everybody wanted a piece of her. Irritated, Erich went outside and followed the path down to the lake.

Kids amused themselves on paddle-boats and called across the water to swimmers in a roped-off section. Birds wheeled in a cloudless sky. Children thundered down the dock, squealing, spitting water, goosing each other. A splash, another splash. Uproarious laughter.

Erich squinted against the brightness, seeing nothing and everything. Here he was. With her. But she was still so far away! Of course he didn't want to make a spectacle of himself, of course she needed time to think, if she was going to reassess her position. Things happened in steps; momentum came gradually. Maybe the goal for the moment was simply to remain a presence, steady, refusing to be erased.

That afternoon, he got the Perfesser, in a session reserved for a lecture by Rodney Barnes. Erich found a seat in the far corner and watched a young woman in snug black cycling shorts set up equipment for a PowerPoint presentation. Soon the places were full. Alison stuck her head in the room, looked around, and then disappeared. A few minutes later, the Perfesser arrived, wearing an infant sling. A curly-haired baby nestled against his belly, legs dangling. *"Ahhh,"* said several of Erich's classmates, "it's Nathalie, look at Nathalie." Clearly they'd already been introduced to the little one.

Rodney disentangled himself from the baby and passed her over to Alison. He was ruddy-faced, no doubt from summer sun on the lake, but otherwise he looked about the same as the last time Erich had seen him. Perhaps more tired, a little thicker around the middle, as befitting a pater familias. "Everyone having a great week?" he asked as he approached the lectern. Rodney didn't wear the same "Embrace Your Aesthetic" T-shirt as everyone else. His shirt was violet and said, "Kiss My Arts." There was a general stirring and affirmative murmur in the group. Yes, this week was great.

He reached for his clicker and the first slide flashed on the screen: A FEW WORDS ABOUT. . .SILENCE.

It turned out to be more than a few words. The slides flipped by, images of classical Roman statuary, mummer plays, masks from Africa, Commedia dell-arte and Japanese Noh theater. Foundational precedents for mime, with which, the Perfesser told them, *"We are sharing a conversation. This week, you have your say!"* He said that a teacher must first and foremost be a good listener, and then he expatiated at length about make-up and its ambiguous function as a mask, as something to hide behind or, on the contrary, as a means to amplify expression. (Erich suspected that Alison had told him of the tension in this morning's class, and the Perfesser was at pains to reassure everyone.) In fairness, Rodney's talk was probably pretty good, but Erich struggled to listen and absorb information. He was too distracted by the sight of Alison with the baby, jiggling it up and down, stroking the top of the child's head, kissing, and soon, holding Nathalie very still in her arms. The little one was asleep.

Suddenly overwhelmed, Erich lowered his eyes to the bare wooden floor. How much could he presume to hope? Was he deceiving himself, indulging in sleight of mind? An artful magic trick broke the rules of nature and fooled you for delight. Life, though, played other kinds of tricks. It fooled you and broke your heart.

Several minutes passed before he could raise his eyes again. Now he observed how Alison's chin touched the baby's head. Her baby. Their baby.

Somehow, she seemed to feel his gaze, and abruptly looked in his direction. He turned away.

The Perfesser was talking about film now, showing desultory excerpts from *Les Enfants du Paradis*. This was followed by Q & A. Surfing on the sound of his own voice, Rodney Barnes didn't even offer the group a bathroom break. At the end of his lecture, when the participants filed out of the room, he surprised Erich by calling to him. "Hi there! Have a minute? Could I speak to you?"

Erich approached the lectern. "Yes?"

"Alison told me that you'd joined us. Everything going all right?"

"Sure."

Erich was conscious of Alison standing not ten feet away, listening to every word. He could also hear Nathalie, who was awake now and had begun to fuss.

"If you need anything," said Rodney Barnes, "and I mean anything at all, don't hesitate to ask me. Okay?"

Erich didn't have the impression that he was being sarcastic. Still, it was a startling thing to hear. Did the Perfesser really imagine that Erich would come to him, as one guy to another, for help? *Advice?* He must be out of his fucking mind. Was the man's ego that big? Erich wouldn't ask him the time of day. In a burning building in a panic in blue smoke, he wouldn't ask Rodney Barnes for the exit. He'd rather take his chances, thank you very much. Jesus! Was Rodney really that stupid?

"Thanks, I'll remember that," Erich said.

"Lise, t'as le sac?"

These words from Alison were directed to the young woman in cycling shorts who'd set up the PowerPoint equipment. She hustled forward with a bag of baby gear. Erich had assumed that she was some kind of camp technician, but now Rodney said, "Erich, this is Lise, our *au pair*."

The young woman flung out her hand, and Erich reflexively shook it, thinking: I really, really have to go. He excused himself and hastened out into the open air.

He left behind the camp complex and plunged down one of the nature trails, seeking distance. For the first hundred yards or so he encountered boisterous children from the puppet theater camp, running on the path or screaming above his head from the limbs of trees. Kids, kids—everywhere! But, eventually, he had the trail to himself, and he pursued it for a long time, until it ended at a craggy granite outcrop like a huge protruding tooth. He clambered atop and discovered an impressive view of Lake Muskalooga and its surrounding forest.

Thoughts caromed around in his head: Baby Nathalie didn't lack attentions, he had to admit. She would be the sort of child who grew up speaking French. Alison wanted that. If he and Alison had stayed together, well, he supposed he could've taught their kid how to manipulate cigarettes. Not quite the same. Oh, it was pointless to indulge in self-pity, but he wanted to scratch the sore, to get back at somebody, even if it turned out to be himself. He vowed that if his turn came someday and he had a child, he would surprise the world and get it *right*, there would be none of the messiness of his past life and his family. He didn't blame his father for running away with another man, his mother for being an alcoholic, or granddad Lou for being a liar. He had blamed them in the past, but not anymore. He knew they'd tried, even as they bumbled. But when his turn came, Erich resolved, he would be as solid as the rock on which he sat. He had a perspective, if only Alison could share it with him!

Mosquitoes appeared with the sunset, so Erich returned to the camp. The smell of ferns was stronger at this hour, a mushroomy funk. At dinner, the cafeteria was eerily quiet. The puppet theater kids were away on a bonfire cook-out, and many of Erich's classmates decided to drive to a nearby town for pizza and beer. "Come join us!" Polly called to him as they headed for the parking area. She held the hand of the young man in low-slung jeans. "We're gonna party."

Erich declined. The idea of a bar scene, and the fact that Alison and the Perfesser would be joining them, made his choice easy.

Late that night, Erich was reading in his cabin when someone knocked on his door. He looked up, startled, and immediately, in spite of everything he'd experienced this day, he wondered: Is it Alison? She'd come to talk to him! He jumped up, wearing only running shorts, and opened the door. To his surprise, it was Doug. The new guy in mime class.

"Yes?" Erich said.

Doug pressed his hands to his chest, then opened outward, for *hello*. He made a sweeping gesture towards Erich's door.

"Christ, give it rest," Erich said. "What do you want?"

"Could I talk to you, Mr. Boots? I won't take up much of your time. But it's very important."

This was strange, but Erich invited him to come in. He offered Doug the chair, and then sat down on the edge of the bed. "Never mind the 'mister'. Just call me Erich."

"I was wondering about the 'Boots', too," replied Doug. "Why that name instead of Ambrose?"

Erich sat up straighter. "Who are you? What do you want?"

"We need you to come back to Chicago. The situation is urgent. We don't know what you're doing up here, but whatever it is can wait. Our priorities are down there."

How did you even find me? Erich wondered. A short time ago, he hadn't known himself that he was coming here. It wasn't his original plan. "I'm confused. You'll have to do some explaining."

"When events move quickly, we have to move with them. If we get left behind, then we're really asking for trouble. *Jesus!*"

He jumped to his feet so abruptly that his chair tipped behind him with a crash. Erich flinched but he also glimpsed Mr. Boots darting under his bed.

"You have rats?" Doug exclaimed, pointing. "That's the biggest rat I've ever seen!"

Erich was tempted to string him along, but he shook his head.

"It's just my rabbit. Don't worry."

"You let it run around in here?"

"He prefers it to his cage." Erich pointed to the box in the corner. Doug picked up his chair and set it aright.

"Well. . .whatever."

"Do you work for Heffernan?" Erich asked. "She hasn't done me any favors."

Doug looked around the room. "I'm not here on her behalf. She hasn't done us any favors."

"So Plutov sent you?"

Doug laughed. "Hardly."

"Who are you? You say 'we' and 'us' but I don't know who you're talking about."

"Your friend Agent Heffernan is concerned with domestic matters. That's what brought her to Andre Plutov. My focus is international. Not the same set of questions."

"So what's that mean? You're CIA? NSA?"

He nodded. "Something like that."

"Like what? Which? Something else? Spell it out for me."

"Our efforts and Agent Heffernan's are complementary. As you can probably imagine, I don't have it written on a business card. I don't wear a sign around my neck. But I can show you this."

He stood, reached into a pocket of his voluminous golf shorts, and extracted a thin black booklet which he handed to Erich. It was a passport and the name said Douglas Jenkins. The photo matched. It was the first time Erich had seen a diplomatic passport.

He handed it back. "How do I know this is real?"

Doug sat down and was quiet for a moment. "I suppose the literal answer is that you don't. But it is."

"I can't see how I could be of help to someone like you.

"Hear me out."

Flowers and Sand

HE FOLLOWING MORNING Erich worked on carrying invisible buckets of sand. They were very heavy! The muscles in his arms strained, his knees trembled as he moved from one point to another. Around him classmates labored at pounding invisible nails, pushing non-existent wheelbarrows and painting walls of empty space. They were building a house.

To his surprise, Erich was enjoying the distraction. He gave himself up to the task. There was a pleasure in learning something new, in making progress. Sure, they were only beginners and dilettantes and, for someone really good at the art, for an accomplished mime, watching them labor would be as gratifying as when Erich watched an amateur perform a dull card trick. On the other hand, no one *owned* an art. Everybody could give it a stab. That was a mercy, in the end.

In a far corner of the room, Doug lifted his arms and spread them slowly, slowly: he was a blossoming flower. He was in a different group. They hadn't spoken since the previous evening in the cabin. In fact, Doug didn't speak to anyone; he'd joined the zealots, who were attempting a more ambitious narrative, trying to piece it together organically, without verbal consultation. They were a garden.

"Looking good!" Alison called. She pointed to a wheelbarrow worker. "But try to keep your back straight. Like this." She walked a semi-circle, her knees half-bent.

Last night, after hearing Doug's proposition, Erich had told him to go to hell. But today, laboring with invisible buckets, he still didn't know what to do.

Doug had said that he needed Erich to deliver a message to Plutov. He was not at liberty to say what the message was, but it was of great importance and proper timing was crucial to its success.

"Deliver it yourself," Erich replied. "Why me? Plutov doesn't even know me."

"He knows who you are. He's aware that you were recommended by Marchenko. He relies on Marchenko but he doesn't trust him, not anymore. And you broke a Marchenko employee's fingers. This has given you a bit of a reputation, Erich. In his eyes you're more than a just an entertainer. He thinks you're with a program. A timely word from you would make a difference."

"Who on earth is Marchenko? What program? Why would you tell me all this?" And as he asked these questions, he silently took note of Doug's phrase *"just an entertainer."* The condescension.

"Marchenko's ex-wife, Yelena, was the one who recommended you to Serena for the birthday party. They go to the same Pilates class. That's what got you in the Plutovs' door. You can probably thank your Agent Heffernan for that."

Erich ran a hand through his hair. "She's no pal of mine. Is the FBI going after Marchenko for back taxes, too?"

Doug's face was blank. "Hard to say. Dunno. If I did know, I couldn't tell somebody like you. You have no clearance. But stop and think for a minute. Everything else I've said is obvious to anyone who is observant. It's not classified. Read a fucking newspaper, Erich. The point is, if you need me to underline, Plutov would see you as Marchenko's bidder. That's interesting. Plutov has cooperated with Marchenko in the past but there was a major falling out. That's common knowledge, too, no big secret. Marchenko isn't one of the good guys. There's no reason to trust the man. So, Erich, you can do the right thing and help your country. And I'd see to it," Doug raised his finger, "that you helped yourself."

"Oh really? So you're the guy who sets everything right?"

Erich fired back without hesitation but he was stalling, trying to absorb what he heard.

"No," Doug said. "I'm here to get things done."

"Good for you. But I don't know anybody named Marchenko. I don't have a dog in this fight. Really. So I'll just leave it to all you smart people. I'm not breaking any laws. As far as I'm concerned, I'm just a kid at summer camp." He nodded toward the door. "You can go now."

Doug didn't move. "I'm your only friend right now, Erich. You say you don't have a dog in this fight, but if you're perceived as having one, it comes down to the same thing. You might as well use it to your advantage. Heffernan's people have their own agenda. You told me yourself that she was no friend. Mrs. Plutov is sour on you. That's why she went behind her husband's back and tried to kick your ass." Erich didn't say a word, but Doug nodded. "That's not over. When Mrs. Plutov is off her meds she wakes up a different person every day. Who knows what she'll try next? So that leaves me, Erich. I'm your only amigo."

"So what do you offer? All I've heard so far is that I should do something for you."

"What do you want?"

This was actually a hard question. He wasn't going to mention money. Now that he'd lost his job at Wendall's and cancelled gigs at the Althea, he'd certainly need a new source of income. But it was like granddad Lou had said. If you accepted money from this kind of person, you could expect more trouble. Wasn't worth it.

"I wouldn't take a dime from you," Erich said.

"How pure." Doug bent down and peered under the bed, where Mr. Boots lurked in the shadows. "There are other options. Right here and now. You chose this place because of her, didn't you? I bet you want to fuck him up, don't you?"

"What?"

"Alison, our teacher in tights." Doug straightened up. "She's hot. I see you staring at her. Must be tough. You two were together for how long? Four years?"

"I'm not going to talk about that."

This turn in the conversation was unnerving. Erich had become accustomed to surprises but he hadn't expected Doug to go *there*. As if his past with Alison was within the reach of a paid sneak with a diplomatic passport.

"Don't tell me you haven't thought about it, dude. You have every reason to dislike Professor Barnes. You want to fuck him up, don't you? Why wouldn't you? That dimblebutt. Doctor Numb Nuts. Want to go after him? There are better ways than getting physical. That's a fact." Doug placed a hand over his heart and then let it drop, as if exhausted.

Erich didn't answer. Yes, there had been a frankly feral period when he'd fantasized physical confrontations with Rodney Barnes. In the months following Alison's departure, Erich had imagined crossing paths with him at a bar and punching him out in front of an appreciative audience (cheers all around!), or bumping into him at a supermarket and sending him flying among cans of tuna. *The Perfesser is going down!* He'd repeated this phrase in his mind, many times. But he'd never acted on such fevers. And this afternoon, seeing and listening to Rodney hadn't made him feel violent, just vaguely ill.

Doug chuckled. "What if Alison heard that her husband was putting the squeeze on that *au pair* with the tasty ass? I bet that would cost the old boy some grief."

"That's nonsense. I don't believe that. Alison wouldn't believe it, either."

"What if the *au pair* herself made the accusation? You think Alison wouldn't entertain doubts?" Now Doug put on a French accent: "'*He keeps standing over me and it makes me uncomfortable. And then he touched my little thigh. Mais oui!*' That's one way to get him."

"I didn't say I wanted to get him, all right? I don't want to hurt her, either. Not Alison. Jesus."

Doug looked at him fixedly. "All right then." He leaned forward. "Flip it the other way. Imagine that it's going to happen, whether you want it to or not. Very unpleasant things are going to reach Alison's ears about her husband. He'll be denounced. It'll be upsetting for her, you can bet on it. Devastating." He touched his chin. "*Dommage, Monsieur Boots!*"

"What are you, twelve years old?"

"No. But I'm in the business of getting things done. I'm not prepared to wait around. Still, there's one way for you to stop it, Erich. Come back to Chicago with me. You'll be rewarded, too."

"You're a twisted fuck. You'd do that? Spread lies and disrupt the life of a couple who have nothing to do with you? They just had a kid, Doug."

"You don't have to like me. But truly I can help you, if you help me. We'll need to leave tomorrow. I'll let you sleep on it. If you don't accept, Alison will be sorry. All because you chose not to stop it, while missing an opportunity to improve your situation."

Erich pointed to the door. "Doug, take the path to the bottom of the hill. It leads to the lake. Go and jump in it."

He slept poorly. Staring into the darkness, he turned over the situation. Was this guy some psycho? Or was it his line of work, another day at the office, as far as he was concerned? If Doug wasn't bluffing and truly meant what he said, Erich could fight back. He could pull Alison aside and warn her. But even to broach the subject was more than distasteful. It made Erich a meddler, the bearer of unwanted news—or worse, he was part of the problem. How much credibility would he have, now that he'd imposed himself on Alison's class and exposed her to the likes of Doug? He'd promised not to make any trouble. But look what followed in his wake!

The following morning in the cafeteria, Doug stood beside him at the coffee urn while he was filling his cup.

"Well, what do you say?"

"I'm still thinking on it."

"We have to leave after lunch."

Erich moved away without answering. Later, during a break in the morning session, people made small talk and Pastor Larry asked Alison, "How's Nathalie today?"

A friendly question, entirely innocent. Alison responded, "Fine. Rodney and Lise are taking her down to Cedar Point. It's a nice trail for a stroller."

Erich glanced at Doug, who saw him and flicked out his tongue. His meaning was lewd and unmistakable.

After the break, Alison introduced the class to some new exercises performed to music. A few minutes into Debussy, suddenly Ron dropped to the floor. "OW! AHH!" He writhed on his side, curling a knee to his stomach. "AHH!"

"What is it?" said T.J.

Alison came forward. "Stand back, everyone. Ron? What happened?"

"My sciatica. Oh, it's terrible. I was afraid this would happen before the gala. I didn't tell anybody." He rolled to his other side.

Ron was very upset. But he managed to rise to one knee and in a quavering voice he made a speech about how even though he was wounded in action, the show must on. Alison let him finish and then told the group that the morning session was done. She would see them in the afternoon.

Outside, Doug said, "Well, amigo? We could head out now."

Erich had made up his mind to leave this place. He'd hoped to say goodbye to Alison, to summon the appropriate words, but she was still inside with Ron and this wasn't a good time. Was there ever a good time? The best thing he could do for Alison was to vanish. "All right." Erich couldn't bring himself to look at Doug. "Meet you in the parking area."

Back at the cabin, he changed out of his "Embrace Your Aesthetic" T-shirt and packed his suitcase. He cornered Mr. Boots and grabbed him by the scruff. He was getting better at catching him, but when he slid the rabbit into the cage and reached to close the door, Mr. Boots nipped at his hand. He only grazed a finger, but Erich cried, "Whoa! What's the matter with you?"

On the path leading to the parking area, he spoke to the wire mesh. "What if I just dumped you here in the woods? Think you could handle that, city rabbit? How about some quality time with the foxes?"

Doug was waiting when Erich emerged from the trees. "Were you talking to somebody?"

Erich shook his head.

Doug drove a big black SUV with massive tires, and he invited Erich to take the lead in his jeep, perhaps in order to keep Erich in his line of vision. After a couple of hours on the road, they turned into a truck stop for a break and a snack.

Facing Doug in a booth, Erich asked a question that had been troubling him.

"How did you find me? I kept my phone turned off and haven't used a credit card. Did someone put a tracking device on my jeep?"

"I don't talk about that stuff."

"I've seen how Heffernan operates. I've helped out on the technical side. I doubt you could say anything that would surprise me."

Doug smiled. "Oh, that so? You're an FBI man, are you?"

"No, I didn't say that."

"Listen, Erich. I'm glad you consented to come along. But let's keep it real. You'll deliver a message—and that's it. Simple. I won't be needing your technical expertise."

He said these last words with a dismissive tone that rankled Erich.

"When they wanted to bug Plutov's house, they sent me in. That's a fact."

"Bullshit," Doug said. "They have their own people for that kind of thing."

Erich proceeded to tell him that he didn't care if Doug believed him or not. The FBI used translucent monitors. They wanted to stick them in every room.

Now Doug shook his head and laughed. "*Translucent monitors?* That's hilarious."

"What?"

Doug feigned looking under the table. "Woooo! But maybe I get it now. Those listening devices aren't for real. It's not so simple. That's gadget bullshit straight out of a bad movie. Translucent? Don't they wish! Heffernan was probably testing you, to see if you were a promising informer. She gives you a task to do, to measure your potential. The FBI works that way a lot. They corner somebody and play good cop/bad cop, they weed out the prospects. It's hit and miss, but it's cheap and sometimes you find a keeper. Somebody you can use on a case. They probably fucked around with the Plutov's pizza delivery boy, in the event he might come in handy someday."

A sour sensation ebbed through Erich's gut.

"Don't feel bad," Doug offered. "I won't waste your time in that way."

"I don't feel bad," Erich lied.

"You were tricked because you wanted to make something better. You wanted to believe. There are worse things."

Back in his jeep, rolling down the highway toward Chicago, Erich asked Mr. Boots, "Tell me. Why is it so easy to hate people?"

SOLDIER FIELD

Improvisation

SOMETIMES you had to improvise. The mark of a fine performer was not only excellent execution but also the ability to make a trick work when something went wrong. No one was flawless. He remembered a story that Fred Cunningham had told him about Bad Fred, back in the days when his wife and two kids resided in a shelter. Bad Fred had secretly sold his wife's car, which is how she lost her job, because she couldn't get to work, and he'd taken the money and gone on a bender. Much of what transpired was lost to his memory due to a blackout, but he returned to his senses one night in a tattoo parlor in Moline, on the banks of the Mississippi, when he found himself sprawled in a chair, aware of a painful burning on his bicep. He looked over and saw an artist applying his needle, outlining a heart. Inside the heart, the letters "T" and "I". He noticed a big woman in a stretchy yellow dress, blowing on her arm. She looked at him and smiled, displayed her bicep, with its welty heart and the name FRED.

Ah yes, he thought. That's Tiny. She calls herself Tiny. It's short for Ernestine.

His arm burned, and he turned to the artist. Suddenly, a thought popped into his head.

Maybe this isn't a good idea.

"Wait a second!" he exclaimed.

The buzzing stopped. "What?"

"Change it."

"Change it? You shitting me?"

Fred looked in panic at Tiny, who was no longer smiling, and then back at his arm. His wife's name was Becky. This tattoo would be hard to explain to her when he made his way back to Chicago and tried to patch things up. Then Fred had an idea. "Make it 'Tony.' You can do that, right?"

"The 'O' is gonna look funny."

"Don't worry about it."

"Who the fuck is Tony?" Tiny demanded.

Fred ignored her, watching his arm, and when he refused to answer her questions, she stomped out of the room. Tony was Fred's son. This would show that he'd been thinking of the family while he was away. But there was also his daughter, Fred recalled. It would look bad to leave out Tabitha. But the heart was only so big. "Could you fit in 'Tabs' beneath that?" he asked.

Years later, Fred showed Erich the tattoo. It was the sorriest specimen of a tattoo he'd ever seen. Bunched up and barely legible. Like a huge smallpox scar.

"Becky and the kids weren't impressed, either," he admitted. "But sometimes you have to improvise! And it got Bad Fred out of a jam."

Doug and Erich reached Chicago that evening and checked in to a motel near the I-94 exit. Doug paid for Erich's room with his credit card, and a young woman at the reception desk said that a package was waiting.

"Excellent!" Doug turned to Erich. "It's our clothes for tomorrow." He signed for a long flat box and tucked it under his arm. "We get to dress up for the party."

In the elevator, Erich asked, "What do you mean, 'party'?"

"It's where we'll see Plutov tomorrow and give him the message. Come by my room in an hour, I'll explain everything. Let's send out for some food. Pizza okay? Pepperoni? Green pepper?"

Erich went to his room and threw down his bag. He made another trip to fetch Mr. Boots, but this time he left him in his cage. He undressed and stepped into the shining bathroom. The powerful showerhead and fluffy white towels felt luxurious after the rudimentary camp facilities.

He could still change his mind, he told himself. Alison was hundreds of miles behind them. He could bolt. Get out of town.

But running away felt like a postponement, not a solution. Neither Serena nor Agent Heffernan offered a way out. But maybe Doug could accomplish it? He was unquestionably a dick, but he didn't try to hide his dickishness. A transaction might be possible.

In Doug's room, they ate hungrily while canned laughter spilled out of the television. Doug was relaxed and cheerful, opening the pizza boxes, acting the host.

"Give me another look at your passport," Erich said.

Doug fished it out and tossed it over.

"Explain to me," Erich asked, studying the photo, then flipping through the pages. "Why should you help me?"

"I said I *could* help you, if you help me. You'll be helping your country, too. It's up to you."

"You could get Heffernan off my back? And I'll never have to deal with the Plutovs again. You could make that happen?"

"Yes, if you hold up your end. Neither of those prospects are incompatible with my objectives, so I could help you." He pointed to the passport. "You done with that?"

Erich toyed with it a little longer, making him wait. "So tell me about this party," he said. "What do I do?"

"It's a dress-up party." Doug put down his slice of pepperoni and reached for the long flat box. He ripped it open and pulled out a black-and-white striped shirt. With a shake, he held it in front of himself, inspecting the size. He dropped it on the bed and pulled out another shirt and threw it to Erich.

"I told them you were a medium. You ever been a referee?"

"Football?" Erich asked.

"You heard of Real Fantasy Football? It's pretty hot right now."

Erich shook his head.

"It's a theme party concept. Basically it's dressing up for rich assholes. Bunch of grown men put on equipment, uniforms, play a game and prance around like the pros. It's especially popular with these fresh foreign millionaires. They think American football is cool. So they organize a friendly game at a nice venue, with plenty of food and booze and the rest. Our friend Plutov is a Bears fan. He's got a bunch of season's tickets, shares them out to impress his pals. And the next step up the social ladder, if that's your thing, is to have a Real Fantasy game. That's what's happening tomorrow. We're not guests but we'll be part of the support staff. I'll be looking out for you, Erich, you won't have anything to worry about. When the time is right, I'll let you know when to approach Plutov and what to say."

Erich swallowed a bite. "Why go to all this trouble? Wouldn't it be simpler just to catch him when he's alone somewhere, say 'Hey' and give him the damn message and be done with it?"

"It's not only words, Erich. It's the *effect*. The task is to get inside someone's head and make sure what he sees. A man like Plutov hears and fears all sorts of things. Here, he's going to be enjoying his private party, his success, surrounded by friends. This is a highlight for him. A cherry on top of the cake. But then you'll appear out of thin air and give him a reminder of his vulnerability, of the fact that he can't insulate himself. He knows you infiltrated his son's party. He knows that you broke a man's fingers. He'll be very surprised to see you, and your reappearance will make him question everybody around him. Who to trust? Plutov's not such a bad fellow, in truth. He can be very helpful to us. But he needs to be nudged."

"If Plutov thinks he has reason to be afraid of me, what's to stop him from messing me up on the spot? Or what if I go home tomorrow and find somebody waiting for me?"

"No, no. Your presence is not that kind of threat. It's psychological. That's the trick. He'll want to put distance. His priority nowadays is to be legitimate and keep his nose clean, as well as the noses of everybody around him." Doug laughed. "Lighten up, Erich. It's a *party*."

The Message

ERICH HAD PLAYED FOOTBALL till his sophomore year in high school. As a boy, he'd gotten his growth early and in his middle-school years, he'd started as a lineman, a solid, sinewy guard with good footspeed. He enjoyed the physical contact, knocking people to the ground. By the time he turned sixteen, though, adolescence had played a trick and other kids had leapfrogged him in their growth. Suddenly opposing linemen outweighed him by twenty or thirty pounds. He took a relentless beating, his forearms were streaked with purple bruises. Halfway through the season, his coach demoted Erich to second-string.

This wasn't a disappointment. It was a relief! He sat on the bench next to his friend Tom Denison where they told stories and laughed and squirted the water bottle. Tom, without question, was the worst player on the team. He'd joined only to appease his father, a football fanatic who knew all the statistics of the Chicago Bears. In his sophomore year, Tom was a third-string split end who couldn't catch a ball and was afraid of falling down. Nobody had a cleaner uniform than Tom Denison.

But, importantly, time on the bench wasn't only horsing around. Under Friday night lights Erich and Tom spoke of other interests, of magic and theater, and they conceived a different destiny. On the bench they'd coined their slogan, *"See you at the top!"*

It sure is a twisted path to get there, Erich thought the next morning as he pulled on the referee's striped shirt. He was supplied with a white cap as well. At Doug's suggestion, they drove back to his apartment in Rogers Park so he could drop off the jeep and unload his suitcase and Mr. Boots. Erich left the travel cage in the kitchen and quickly inspected his place. Everything appeared untouched since his departure for Wisconsin.

Erich descended the steps of the duplex and climbed into Doug's SUV where baroque string music flowed from the speakers. They rode for several minutes without talking.

Doug said eventually, "Kick-off is at noon."

"Where's the game?"

"Soldier Field."

A feeble joke, Erich thought. A bunch of duffers weren't going to need a 60,000 seat stadium for their party. But he said nothing and listened to the music. Near Argyle Street, Doug suddenly pulled over at an Italian bakery. The narrow space was too small for the SUV, but he nosed forward as far as he could and then opened his door and jumped out. "I'll be just a minute." He left the engine running.

Erich watched him disappear inside the storefront. He glanced uneasily from side to side. What was this about? He reached for his door handle but then Doug trotted out and climbed back behind the wheel. "Okay. Let's go."

For the rest of the ride, Doug was more communicative. "You'll blend in with the caterers. They're all dressed like us. Nobody will pay attention to you. Everybody will be watching the players. Your job is easy-peasy."

"So what's my message?"

Erich had the distinct impression that Doug had only just now learned the message, in the bakery.

"I'll let you know when the time is right."

Erich looked out his window. They were cruising down Lake Shore Drive, past Navy Pier.

"So where are we going?" he asked.

"I told you. Soldier Field."

The stadium loomed large and presently they passed the neoclassical columns. Doug put on his blinker. Now he drove slowly, keeping an eye out for bicyclists and joggers. Erich was astonished. In all his years in Chicago, he'd been inside the stadium only a couple of times in the off-season, to attend rock concerts. "What's it cost Plutov to rent this place for a private event?"

"More money than he needs," Doug said. "And no sense of shame."

They parked in a security lane, remarkably close to the entrance. It felt like driving up onto the sidewalk in front of City Hall. Nearby, behind the open trunk of a car, a portly man was adjusting the thigh pads in a very snug pair of football pants, struggling because his stomach got in the way and he couldn't see what he was doing.

"Since Plutov has gone this far," Erich said, "you'd think he could've rented the Bears' clubhouse, too."

"I suspect he tried."

A security guard with a walkie-talkie greeted them at the stadium gate; Doug handed him a paper. The guard waved them in.

They passed through a tunnel and when they emerged on the level of the playing field, the perfectly trimmed green gridiron was so bright that it made Erich blink. Light had an unfamiliar intensity and an inexplicable feeling of gladness came over him. A few players loped along the sidelines or chatted with hands on hips. A young, helmetless guy with dreadlocks set a ball on a tee, took several steps back, then charged forward and sent a booming kick to the opposite end zone.

"Wow," said Erich. "Doesn't look like an amateur to me."

"They usually bring in a few college players to join them for Real Fantasy," said Doug. "It ups the game."

Caterers in striped shirts were setting up tables and laying out chafing dishes. Cheerleaders strolled up and unzipped sports bags, extracting pompoms. These women were implausibly voluptuous, their costumes skimpier than typical cheerleader outfits. Erich watched them. Perhaps porn actresses hired for the event? They stood by listlessly and waited for something to happen.

"Morning!" A man dressed in white, with a dark belt and black cap and carrying a first-aid kit, stepped forward and shook Doug's hand. "Erich," Doug said, "I'd like you to meet Wayne. Wayne, this is Mr. Boots." They shook hands. Wayne's face was smiling and pink. Doug added, "Wayne is our trainer today. He'll stay with you and keep an eye on things. You're helping out as his assistant. I'll be on the field. Be back in a minute."

Doug jogged away and Erich wondered: So Wayne is my minder? Doug hadn't mentioned him earlier. Wayne waved at the cheerleaders. "*Heyyy!*"

"Hey," a few responded, waving back.

He called again, and this time the cheerleaders ignored him. A few families were unfolding lawn chairs. Erich looked up at the grandstands, tens of thousands of empty seats and sunlight reflecting off the vacant skyboxes. Suddenly he felt very small and insignificant. The vacancy was oppressive. He squinted at the highest rows and imagined snipers.

By now, maybe ninety or one hundred people were present in the cavernous stadium. Doug returned, carrying a net bag full of squeezy water bottles. He leaned close to Erich.

"Do you see him?" he asked.

"Who?"

"Plutov. Over there, in the end zone. Number 12. He just arrived. It's part of the protocol, to make everybody wait for him."

Erich cast his eyes in that direction. Yes—it was Andre Plutov all right, a fire plug of a man in shoulder pads. Helmetless, he tossed a ball with another player. Plutov was pudgy and visibly unfit but his movements possessed a certain kind of grace. Once, when the ball fell short and skidded at his feet, instead of bending over to pick it up, he kicked it neatly back. Obviously he'd played soccer in his youth.

Then Erich spotted Serena Plutov. She stood beyond the goalposts, wearing a Bears jersey and a pair of sunglasses atop her head. The jersey was large and hung down like a mini-dress, exposing her slim legs. She was speaking to her son Viktor, who wore headphones and kicked at the grass in front of him. Erich reached up and pulled the bill of his cap an inch lower.

Doug suggested that he and Wayne take a walk to the other end of the field. Here they idled for a few minutes among players who warmed up or scrolled on cell phones. Many of the men had shaved heads, or affected an otherwise fearsome look, but they put on mock-respectful voices and kidded with their fellows in referee shirts, "Don't be mean to us. *Please.*"

Then Andre Plutov strolled toward the center of the field, followed by his family. A portable P.A. system was wheeled out to the 50 yard line. He took the microphone.

"This is a special day. Our ninth wedding anniversary. We thank all our beautiful friends. You are special people. We celebrate many days! Come here!"

He beckoned to Serena and she stepped forward, pulling along Viktor. Everyone applauded and Erich clapped, too. Serena seemed reluctant to take the microphone, but then she accepted it and said simply, "Let's have a good time. Thank you, everyone, for coming. God bless." More applause and then, after a brief static burst, a recorded version of the national anthem crackled over the portable sound system.

In the immensity of the stadium, the music floated in and out of hearing, as if buffeted by invisible currents. The effect was spooky, with the palpable absence of thousands in a grotesque, empty cathedral. At the final bars, players began to clap and shout and whistle. The cheerleaders bounced on the sideline. "We are the Honeybears!"

Doug leaned in. "We'll let Plutov have his fun. But during the half-time break, I'll set up a moment where you can talk to him. He'll come to you, and you give him the message. Take your time and make sure he recognizes you.

The game will resume, and we'll go home. The message is easy to remember. Here it is: *'All of the people, all of the time.'* Got it?"

Erich nodded, and repeated to himself:

"All of the people, all of the time."

The Real Fantasy

THE ENSUING GAME was a sloppy, light-hearted affair. Both teams wore Bears jerseys, in contrasting black and white, the uniforms for home or away. Doug was the sole referee, running up and down the field, and he appeared competent and in control. Andre Plutov played quarterback for his squad, working out of a shotgun formation, and he attempted a few wobbly, incomplete passes. Both teams were helped by a pair of conspicuously fit players, no doubt the college guys. One of them caught a lateral pass from Plutov and smashed through the line, plowing over tacklers and breaking into open field. Instead of sprinting to the end zone, though, he obligingly circled back and let himself get caught, giving his tacklers a second chance. Spectators clapped and laughed, at least those who were watching; other people were busy filling their plates at the buffet line.

"Hey, give us a hand, will you? We're running low on chicken wings."

It was a young man in a striped shirt from the catering crew. He was talking to Erich.

"No," said Wayne.

"Huh? What do you mean, no?" Clearly he didn't like this answer. He thought that Erich belonged with food service.

"We're busy," said Wayne. "He's with me."

"You're not busy. You're just standing around."

"How 'bout I stick those chicken wings up your ass?" Wayne glared and the young man retreated, glancing nervously over his shoulder.

"Was that necessary?" Erich asked.

"I'm looking out for you, Mr. Boots."

During the game, Erich didn't keep track of the score, which was ridiculously high. *All of the people, all of the time.* The words sounded vaguely familiar—maybe part of an advertising jingle? He must've heard it somewhere. He'd figured that dirty business intrigues nowadays were mainly a matter of bank codes and digital mischief. There was something quaint and old-fashioned about this kind of communication. Erich felt a flippy sensation in his belly, a tingling in his hands, such as he experienced before an important performance.

On the opposite side of the field, Serena and Viktor perched on folding chairs. Serena had lowered her sunglasses, which covered much of her face, and Viktor didn't join the children playing on the sideline turf. It was the first time since the birthday party that Erich had had a chance to observe the boy. Then, with the fiasco of the Shanghai Mystery Box, he'd felt irritation and exasperation. Today, though, he found himself feeling sorry for him. Why didn't he join the others? Serena occasionally bent toward her son to say something, which he sometimes acknowledged. Other times he fidgeted.

No, these people weren't having fun. Why? Erich wondered. Why is it so hard? Look at this party! What more does it take? Why can't they figure it out?

When the whistle blew for half-time, players left the field to mingle with family and friends, removing helmets and making their way to the drinks table. *Pop! Pop!* Bottles foamed, glasses were extended. A beer keg was also in great demand.

Erich and Wayne watched from a distance and, as Doug jogged over to them, Erich became aware of a distant, percussive sound, growing louder, a *chunk-chunk-chunk*. He looked up and saw a helicopter circling the upper reaches of the stadium.

"Give me one of those." Doug pointed to the water bottles at Erich's feet. He was redfaced, sweaty. Erich tossed him a bottle and he took a long drink.

The helicopter began a slow descent. Children at the dessert buffet, fat men in uniform gripping champagne flutes, cheerleaders in spandex and caterers dragging trash bags along the sidelines, stopped what they were doing and lifted their gazes. The helicopter came to rest midfield, the engine roaring before abruptly cutting off. The propeller blades spun and chopped quiet gulps of air.

"Helicopter rides are part of the post-game entertainment," Doug said. "You get a nice view of the lake."

Guests streamed onto the grass to take selfies in front of the helicopter. Others put an arm around a Honeybear's waist and told friends to take a shot. Doug added, "I told Plutov there's a surprise waiting for him from his friends. He thinks it's about an anniversary gift. He agreed to meet up by the goalposts in five minutes. He'll come solo, without his wife. You say your bit, give him the message—and then we head straight for the exit. Same way we came in. Got it?"

Erich nodded, eager to discharge his task and leave this place. On his way to the goalposts, he skirted the melee of partiers. Then he waited. And he waited some more. Erich contemplated the end zone grass, and imagined Mr. Boots nibbling there. Finally Plutov waddled up, the front of his jersey untucked, a smile on his face. "Now what's this all about?"

"Hello. May I have a word?"

"Yes. What is it?"

"Nice to see you again."

Plutov looked at him, but there was no recognition. Erich removed his cap, feigned to wipe his brow against the heat. "It's not easy to choose the right rabbit, is it?"

"What?"

"Remember? We had a little rabbit situation? You told me you'd take care of it? Surely you haven't forgotten me."

For several seconds, Plutov did not reply. "Why are you here?" he said eventually. His expression clouded and his voice was steely. "You are not here to talk about a rabbit."

"That's right. I got a message for you." Erich replaced his cap. *"All of the people, all of the time."'*

Plutov didn't respond, as if waiting for something else. But when Erich added nothing, his face seemed to sag and soften. The effect, however, wasn't to make him look older. Rather, he oddly reminded Erich of a child, of Viktor—the resemblance was very strong. "Now?" Plutov asked. "This you tell me now?"

"That's it," Erich said.

"You go to hell."

Plutov walked away.

Erich didn't linger. He headed straight for the exit tunnel, where Doug and Wayne waited for him. He expected questions but as soon as they saw him, they started moving, too. Caterers wheeled carts ahead of them, a player in uniform came along behind. There was plenty of traffic. Emerging into the sunlight, Erich climbed into Doug's SUV. He waited while Doug and Wayne exchanged a few words on the other side of the vehicle. It was all a sorry charade, Erich thought, and for what purpose? And how much of the trouble outside the stadium was also a sham, with fools in costume scoring empty points? Enough, Erich thought, SOS! It was broiling in the SUV and he rolled down his window.

Suddenly, his head was gripped from both sides. Erich jerked upward in his seat. His cap flew off and his knee slammed up against the dashboard.

"*Motherfucker!*" said a voice.

Fingers pressed vise-like against his cheekbones, pulling him backward. The angle hurt his neck, he arched his back, squirming. Someone was trying to pull him out of the car window—or maybe pull off his head.

Erich shouted and clawed at the hands. His legs kicked and banged against the dashboard and he saw the interior roof of the SUV, side-glints of the windshield, his head swimming in a soup of sounds, of yelling voices. Then he heard screams, and suddenly the vise on his skull let go. He fell hard against the car door. The screaming continued, and he realized that he wasn't the source.

"Erich, come on!" Doug urged.

Above him, he saw two hands wedged between the window and the door frame, with spiderish fingers twitching.

"Get out!" Doug said.

The hands were trapped by the upper edge of the window glass. The automatic window had been raised as high as it could go, and it was still pressing upward. On the other side, a man screamed and banged his knees against the door panel. The door shook. Somehow the hands didn't appear real—they were blotching purple in places, the circulation cut off, and two fingernails were scabbed and oily black. They looked rubbery and gluey like the fake hands that Erich had owned as an adolescent, when he performed with a wrist guillotine.

Doug tugged at him. "Move, Erich! Come out this side."

Now he followed, scrabbling across the front seats of the SUV, and he would've fallen on his face on the asphalt if Doug and Wayne hadn't caught him by the shoulders. The howling continued on the other side of the SUV while they trundled Erich into Wayne's car. "Get out of here," Doug said. "I'll take care of this guy. Bye."

He slammed the door and Wayne's car spurted away, squealing as it turned out of the security lane and into the street. There was a red light at Lake Shore Drive, and they jerked to a halt. Wayne turned to him and grinned. "Where to?"

Amigos

THAT NIGHT Erich ran an errand, and when he came home and moved toward his door, Doug stepped out of the shadows. Just seconds ago, the space had seemed clear. It was as if he'd emerged out of a crack in the ground.

"Jesus! You startled me."

"Where were you?" Doug asked.

"What? Never mind. Just an errand."

"Wanted to check up on you. Telephone is not my thing. You okay? Today finished up a bit rough. Sure you're all right?"

"Nothing major," Erich said.

In truth he was very sore, and it was getting worse. Minutes ago, driving home, he'd found it difficult to turn his head and look both ways before crossing intersections. He had to move his shoulders and pivot his torso, straining against his seatbelt. That afternoon, after Wayne dropped him off and he stumbled upstairs and looked in the bathroom mirror, he found a long trickle of blood going down his jaw and under his shirt. The upper corner of his right ear was torn. He cleaned it up and applied a bandage, also noticing raspberry spots on his cheekbone. Finger marks. By the time he stepped out of his apartment, the bruises had started to turn blue.

"I want to thank you," Doug said. "We got the job done. And don't worry about that guy in the parking lot. He's in the county jail tonight. Criminal mischief and drug charges." He smiled. "Somehow a large amount a fentanyl was found in his gear. Damn shame, huh? We left your name out of it."

"You're full of shit, Doug. You said Plutov wouldn't retaliate."

"He didn't. That guy was acting on his own. I'm surprised he was there. He's a lowlife, not a friend of the family they'd invite to their party. Plutov probably used him to fill out his offensive line. He must've spotted you when you were mingling with the rabble before kick-off. I guess he's still pissed off about his fingers."

"Uh huh."

"It had nothing to do with our job. It wasn't on the program."

"Is that supposed to make me feel better?"

"I've reviewed the film and Plutov didn't have a chance to speak to him after you identified yourself." Doug reached out as if to pat Erich's shoulder but Erich swatted his hand away.

"You filmed this game?"

"Of course. For the record."

Erich felt bone-weary. Suddenly it occurred to him that this evening, at this very minute, a mime show was underway in the Wisconsin woods near Lake Muskalooga, and he was missing it. Those exercises at camp seemed like a long time ago. *Express Your Aesthetic.* Build an invisible house. Well, it beat almost getting your head torn off.

"The main thing," Doug said, "is we got the job done. That's the big picture. I won't trouble you further and rest assured, I'll hold up my end of the bargain. Your service won't be forgotten."

He extended his hand. After a moment's hesitation, Erich shook it.

"Good night, amigo," Doug said.

The Denisons

"**S**O," TOM ASKED, "what's new in your life?"

Thursday night at the Denisons was a cook-out in their back yard. Tom Senior stood at the grill in an apron that said "Hot Diggity Dog!" Mrs. Denison was laying out condiments on the patio table. With both of Tom's parents within earshot, Erich spoke only of his trip to Wisconsin. "Had a change of scene. It was nice."

"Is that where you got hurt?" Mrs. Denison asked.

Erich laughed, touching his cheek. "Yeah, I was unloading a canoe and decided to catch it with my face. I'll know better next time."

He'd been invited to spend the night, too, but intended to stay only for supper. He watched Tom set up a mosquito repellent coil on a ledge of brick. Tom struck a match, and the coil began to smolder.

"Tell him your news, Tom," his father said.

"Yes, tell him!" said his mother.

Tom kept his eyes on the coil. "This one is eucalyptus scented," he mused. Then he added, as if an afterthought: "I've been offered a job in Montevideo. You know—Uruguay?"

He chewed on his lip.

"Wow," Erich said. "No kidding?"

"My company's opening an office down there. They want me to go."

"He would be in charge," said Mrs. Denison.

"Good money, too," said his father.

"Congratulations!" said Erich.

"Thanks," Tom said softly.

It was a warm evening and the Denisons were drinking gin and tonics; Erich sipped a glass of lemonade. Tom Senior became garrulous, telling about the time he'd been to Argentina. "You call these steaks?" He forked a slab of meat and held it up. "This is a kiddie portion compared to what they eat down there!" He slapped it back on the grill, where it sizzled and tongues of flame licked upward. "And not just beef, either. They do this open pit thing where they take an entire lamb and instead of turning it on the spit, they mount it vertically, so it looks like the little guy is crucified? Boy, was that good! People are so friendly, too. And the music!" His feet did a little shuffle on the grass.

"I didn't get to go on that trip," said Mrs. Denison.

Tom Senior stopped shuffling. He looked down at his glass and shook the ice cubes. "It was for work."

After the meal, Erich joined them for a game of lawn darts. The Denisons were competitive and kept score. The darts were preserved in their original box, which dated back to the 1980s and featured a photo of a family with frizzy blow-dried haircuts. "Nowadays these are illegal," Tom Senior told him, holding a bouquet of darts in his fist. "Too dangerous. You ever play?"

Erich admitted his inexperience. Tom Senior chuckled and let fly a dart, spearing a target ring on the lawn. "What can I say? Live free or die."

It was late in the evening before Erich had a chance to speak to Tom in private. They'd retired to the den to watch the final innings of the White Sox game. Tom seemed distracted and moody. "So," Erich began, "You're not too thrilled about Montevideo, are you?"

Tom was defensive. "Well, it's not like I can live with Mom and Dad forever, is it? I never intended to. But Uruguay is a hell of a long distance."

"Oh, I hear you. Of course you don't have to accept the offer. Find something else."

"Like what?"

Tom's mouth rounded into a petulant puff, and Erich understood that he should go gently. Tom had other considerations that went beyond a job. He'd made his life here. He had roots. Loved ones. Lawn darts.

Tom changed the subject. "That was really something about your real estate guy, wasn't it? I didn't want to bring it up in front of Mom and Dad. But with him gone, it might take some of the pressure off you. I mean with your FBI lady."

"Gone? What do you mean?"

"Well, they killed him, right? Nice bunch of people, that's all I can say."

"Are you talking about Plutov?"

Tom rubbed the back of his neck. "You messing with me? Come on, it's all over the news. You live in a cave or what?"

"*Who?* Who killed him?"

On the drive to the Denisons' house, Erich had listened to his I-pod, not the radio. He hadn't been online since early that morning.

"Some Russians I guess. Maybe the government. Who knows? He got shot in a toilet in a fancy restaurant in Moscow. That's all they're saying. Here, this game is boring." Tom picked up the remote control and flicked to a news channel, and then he tried another, but other stories were running, so they took out their phones and did subject searches. The stories were inconclusive about the circumstances and perpetrators, just as Tom had said, but they all agreed on the central fact. Photos showed a younger man than the one Erich had encountered.

"Andre Plutov, 51, of Wilmette, Illinois, was found dead late Wednesday in Moscow's famed Blue Blossom restaurant. A police statement released Thursday morning said that an employee discovered his body in the washroom and immediately contacted emergency services. The cause of death was multiple gunshot wounds. No arrests have been made, but an investigation is in progress.

"Plutov, who was born in Kaluga, had lived in the United States for 14 years, a successful entrepreneur and generous contributor to Chicago civic organizations. He is survived by his wife and one child."

Erich slumped in his chair. "I can't believe it. I just saw this guy. I just spoke to him. And now he's dead over there?"

"No shit? What did you talk about?"

Erich ignored him, scrolling on his phone. The accounts were similar though some included photos of Serena, too, looking glamorous, and in one shot she was very sweet and innocent, wearing a tiara, a heartland queen.

"Fuck."

"Tell me," Tom persisted. "What did you talk to him about? What happened?"

Erich looked up. Earlier in the day, he'd anticipated telling him about the party at Soldier Field. He wanted to share the weirdness of it all, to vent his disbelief at the spectacle and the desperation. But now he felt implicated in something terrible. It was nothing to dismiss.

"Oh, it was just in passing. Not like I know the guy and we have much to talk about." He looked back down at his screen, pressing his fingers to his temple. "Says here he arrived in Moscow on Sunday. By himself."

"Someone must've booked him a one-way ticket."

The Last Interview

WAS HE MORE entangled now? Or less? His assailant was locked up. Plutov was dead. Serena was on her own now, and graspers from all sides were surely busy with the question of Plutov's money. If the FBI had been focused on his financial dealings, then the case had taken a complicated twist. Erich wasn't surprised when Agent Heffernan telephoned him.

"Say, could you come down to the office? Today if possible. Or tomorrow morning. Does that work for you?"

Her tone was solicitous.

Erich took a breath, forced himself to wait a moment. "What's it about?"

"You must've heard the news."

"Uh huh."

"This should be our last interview. I sure hope so."

That was encouraging, wasn't it? Erich immediately pushed their meeting to the next day in order to give himself more time to think; but shortly after putting down the phone, a restlessness came over him about having to wait. What would she say?

He looked pensively out the window at Bonnie Kubek's back yard, which was overgrown and neglected. He tramped downstairs and went to work, cutting and trimming and weeding, hoping the physical activity would grant him mental clarity. Or at least distract him. He ripped out creeping ivy along the fence line and groomed the spot of Spud's grave, all the while turning over events in his mind.

Doug had spoken of Plutov in almost friendly terms. Putting aside the FBI investigations about money and allowing for the fact that anything Doug said might be a calculated falsehood, was it possible that Plutov had been cooperating with Doug's people, informing or serving as a conduit for information about his contacts, in the U.S. or back in Russia? He worked for the Americans? Or was it the opposite, and Doug had intentionally set up Plutov for what happened to him in Moscow? Or Doug wasn't responsible but people in Moscow had come to mistrust Plutov for their own reasons, and they'd resorted to desperate measures? Any of these scenarios seemed possible. There were conceivably others, too. But for all their contradictions, they shared a common foundation of opportunistic lies.

Erich scraped a rake toward a pile of torn vines. He was working fast.

Plutov was some kind of thug, but he'd done Erich no harm. No—wait—Plutov had actually tried to *help* him. His rabbit scheme hadn't worked, but he'd acted to improve Erich's situation, and he hadn't asked for anything in return.

And what did I do for him? Erich asked himself, his hair and shirt soaked with sweat, a droplet sliding to the tip of his nose. *I had sex with his wife. I physically injured his son. And then I gave him a message that sent him running out of town, toward his death.*

The droplet fell.

Maybe, he thought ruefully, if Tom Denison goes Montevideo, he'll need an assistant?

The morning of the interview with Agent Heffernan, Erich was twenty minutes late. He'd left his apartment at a reasonable hour but traffic was bad. He limped into her office—he'd banged his knee pretty hard on the dashboard of Doug's SUV, and it seemed to be getting worse, not better, as he climbed the stairs. "I was beginning to wonder if you were going to stand me up," she said.

Erich sat before her, slightly out of breath, his heart thumping. "I keep my word. How are you doing?"

She lifted her glasses on the chain and put them on her nose. "Kind of you to inquire. Fine, thank you." He could tell that she was noticing the marks on his cheek. "But we can't say the same for our friend Plutov, can we?"

Erich shook his head. But he didn't volunteer any words.

Agent Heffernan continued, "I have some news for you. I didn't want to say it on the phone. Better to see you personally. It's good news."

He waited. "Yes?"

"It turns out that Bonnie Kubek left a will. We didn't know about it before. And you're mentioned in the will, Erich. In fact, you have inherited the entire property. You have the right to live there. You haven't broken any laws. The place has been yours all along!"

Erich's ears drummed as if he were underwater. He straightened in his chair. "What? Really?"

She studied him for a moment, and then snorted. "Hell no! That was a joke, kid. You *are* easy to fool. Jesus!" She rocked back in her chair. "That's always been the trouble with you." She smiled, pleased with herself. "Have to take my laughs where I can get them. You must live in a fairy tale land."

"No, I don't. But I should know better than to trust your word."

"I'm not going to miss you, Ambrose. Your attitude has been a pain in the ass from the start."

Erich no longer knew what to say. But he was certain of this much: her sneer was sincere.

"The real reason I called you in here," she continued, "is to let you know that I have been relieved of this case. *Moved.* And you are no longer considered a person of interest. It's a curious thing. Especially the timing. In all my career I've seen nothing quite like it. It's counter-productive and I've made it clear to my superiors that I think so. But that's the situation and I can't change it. You and I are finished. Your file is closed. We won't be seeing each other anymore."

"Sounds like a win-win."

"But before I go, I have to ask. Is there any last thing you want me to know? Think it over before you answer."

Erich allowed for an appropriate pause, but he had no doubt about his reply.

"Nope."

"If somebody is looking out for you, Erich, all I can say is you'd better be careful. You might not like it."

"Listen," he said, "I just want to be left alone. That's the God's truth."

"Then get out of my office."

A Time for Eggs

OUR MIND COULD ONLY take in so much. On the drive home, while stopped at a red light, he watched the people crossing in front of him: office workers and slow-moving seniors, tourists in baggy T-shirts, a kid with ear-buds rolling by on a skateboard. Going about their business. As if the world were a sensible, decipherable place. Maybe it was an illusion necessary to survival.

He took out his cell phone.

"Fred? Hey, it's Erich. Feel like going out for eggs?"

"I was worried about you. You back in town? You okay?"

"Yeah. So—you up for eggs?"

"It's almost noon. I had my breakfast."

"So order something else. Make it lunch."

"All right. But can you drive me? My car got stolen."

"No problem. Ten minutes?"

"All right."

The light changed, Erich drove on. Soon he saw Fred waiting at the curb, wearing a blue track suit. Probably from the free bin at the Salvation Army, but it actually fit him pretty well. He looked svelte. Fred folded himself slowly into the jeep and gave Erich a pat on the arm. "There's my man."

"Yo." He put the jeep in gear and headed for Thurston's Diner, hitting a string of green lights on the way. "Sorry to hear about your car. Who needs that shit?"

Fred shrugged. "Well, I've been a little shaky, you know? With the fainting spells. Maybe it's not so good me driving anymore. And I collect on the insurance, too!" he added brightly. "Good timing all around."

At Thurston's, they took a sunny booth where they could watch the street. Erich ordered his eggs and bacon and lump of feta cheese. He waved the menu and tried to tempt Fred with a pulled pork sandwich, but in the end Fred reverted to breakfast, and ordered pancakes. "Tall stack," he told the waitress, grinning lasciviously with his chipped tooth, "with a side of ham."

Their order dispatched, they sat in silence for a moment, basking in rays of light.

"Thanks for coming out, Fred."

"My pleasure. Anytime is a good time for eggs. What happened to your face? Jealous husband?"

The waitress returned with their coffees and cutlery wrapped in paper napkins.

"Unfortunately, no," Erich said. "Let me get some food in and I'll tell you. What's new in Fredworld? How's Manny? Getting better?"

Fred shook his head. "That's what happened to my car. Haven't seen him since. But I can't prove it, so I haven't mentioned him to the cops. Manny still has some things to figure out, you see. The kid has to step up to the plate. How 'bout you? Keepin' healthy? Still in the ballgame?"

"Yeah."

"Good man."

"You?"

Fred nodded, working a fingernail in his ear. "Thanks for askin'."

When their food arrived, Fred dumped a prodigious amount of syrup on his cakes, sawed off gluey hunks and happily stabbed them between his lips. Erich ate more slowly. Pensive, he looked out the window.

Fred said, "Well, I'll say this much for you. You done good."

Erich swallowed, then laughed. "Really? Why do you say that?"

"I was worried. Last time I saw you, I smelled trouble. You were pretty worked up. I got your back, but in the end it's up to you. And now you're here where you belong. I'm proud you're doing so well."

They ate in silence for a while.

"Thanks Fred. But it doesn't always feel that way. Far from it."

"Feelings are conniving little fuckers. They make the world shrink. I mean pain, that's what I'm talking about, those kinds of feelings." He pointed with his fork. "You bang your shin, *yah, whang!* Brother, that's all there is. In that moment the pain blinds you. The world becomes as small as the room you're limpin' around in. It just hurts. You can't see the big world outside, which is waitin' for you with lots of good things. That's where the eggs and everything else is. You can't forget that. Otherwise you end up like Bad Fred. Bad Fred spent his time running around a small room."

"Hard to run with banged-up shins."

"Even worse when you're blind."

"You bump into more stuff?"

"My point exactly!"

The conversation played out in this way. They'd had similar conversations before, bordering on nonsensical. They were circling something unsayable, and the only way to express it was to draw this circle around it.

"And now you get to buy me breakfast," Fred said. "You're one lucky son-of-a-bitch."

This, too, was the sort of thing Erich had heard before. It was one Fred's standards. *Go out and do something for somebody. You owe it to yourself.* Erich more or less believed him but he was often slow to act on this belief. Sipping his coffee, Erich wondered how he would say goodbye to this man he loved.

Because that's what this breakfast was really about, wasn't it? If he was going to leave the room—which he should've done long ago!—he couldn't do so without properly saying goodbye to Fred. He wished for a better way to honor him than a plate of pancakes.

But first, he'd have to explain why he was leaving. He took a breath—and then told Fred everything, pausing only when the waitress came to re-fill their cups, then resuming when she was out of earshot. Fred listened in silence. "I don't know if it was our side or their side that killed this guy, or if it was an accident, a plan that went wrong. I'm not sure even the higher-ups know exactly, or would agree among themselves about who's responsible. These people aren't as smart as they think they are. But this much I do know, and it has nothing to do with grubby politics or somebody's career: I saw a kid spend his last day with his father without knowing it was his last day. Before he lost him. And Fred, I helped make it happen. I didn't *want* that, but there's no way I can undo it. God, I should've got out of the room earlier." Erich threw down a wadded paper napkin. "So fuck me."

Fred didn't bat an eye.

"And you were sober when all this shit went down?"

"I told you I was," Erich snapped. "That's not the point."

"Well yes and no, no and yes." Fred ran a finger on his plate for some syrup. "That's quite a little story you got there. It don't have to make sense, I mean not in the way to satisfy a lawyer." He stuck his finger in his mouth. "Maybe you messed up, okay. But look at it this way. You *know* you messed up. That makes you not an asshole. Hear me? You got your health, you're free, you're sober. The way I see it, you're holding three aces. You're not out of the woods 'cause the dealer holds the fourth ace, but still, Erich, you're in a position to do better."

"You think I can trust Heffernan and Doug and that crowd?"

Fred shook his head. "Naw. Dealer's crooked. But it sounds like their game has moved on, as far as you're concerned."

Erich wanted to believe him. Fred shifted in the booth. "Say, whatever happened to that crazy rabbit?"

"I didn't tell you that part of the story, did I?"

Late on Saturday night, after the real fantasy at Soldier's Field, Erich had performed a final errand. He was sore and confused and drove past his destination several times as he planned his final step. He parked around the corner and moved swiftly, clutching a pillow case.

He paused in front of the house, glancing in both directions. The house was dark, but in the living room window Erich could see the blue glow of a TV screen. He moved swiftly up the steps, put down the pillow case in front of the door, and pressed hard on the doorbell, several times. Then he jumped down and hurried away.

From behind a neighbor's hedge, Erich watched the steps. A light switched on. The front door opened. There was a silence, and then an exclamation: *"Oh my, it's you! Thank God! It's really you!"*

Erich returned to the jeep and drove away.

"So Mr. Boots made it home," Fred raised his coffee cup as if for a toast. The waitress brought the bill.

"Yeah, that's right. Mr. Boots got away with it."

Fred grinned. "Show me a trick."

EPILOGUE

Baldwin Hills

I T WASN'T MONTEVIDEO, but Los Angeles was a major change, nonetheless. You could leave the room without leaving the country. After six years, Erich was comfortable in calling California home.

A few days after his breakfast with Fred Cunningham, the telephone rang at midnight. Erich was in bed but still awake, his laptop propped on his knees, looking at websites and chat pages about Seattle and Portland. These were attractive places nowadays. If he moved, which was more promising? Or maybe Ashland? The phone jangled, startling him—he sat up straight. He didn't recognize the caller ID. He took a deep breath. His first thought was of Serena Plutov. Was he still on her list? How was she coping with her husband's death? What could he say to her now? He answered curtly.

"This is Erich."

"Yes, hello?" came a tremulous voice. "How are you? I've been meaning to get in touch."

It was Jerry Teasdale. Erich hadn't heard from him in ages. When was the last time they'd spoken? Christmas? "Hey Jerry. I didn't recognize your number."

"My old phone melted on the patio. Still can't scrape off the stain. How are you doing, Erich?"

Where to begin? Erich's mind raced ahead, considering possibilities. In less than a minute, after the usual niceties, he redirected the conversation. "You know, you've mentioned a couple of times that we should get together? Well, I've been thinking. The timing might be right on my end, if I could take you up on your hospitality. . ."

Jerry sounded surprised but he made no objection. "Uh, okay. You can stay as long as you need. I got an upstairs room. Sure, Erich. Come to Weebanks!"

Weebanks, Erich soon discovered, wasn't the California of glamorous images. A tiny desert town southeast of Palm Springs, between a military base and the Salton Sea, it was a desolate hamlet with a lunar landscape. There was *nothing* to do there. Even the lizards moved slowly, moping around in a half-assed way, as if they'd given up caring 40,000 years ago. Temperatures soared to enervating heights in daytime and at night, it could get quite chilly. Occasionally fighter jets ripped across the sky, assaulting your ears and leaving vapor trails. They came from a military base at the foot of the mountains, a sector strictly off limits to the public but ever palpable in the distance, with rumbling and resonating booms. For Jerry Teasdale, Weebanks was a cheap place to retire after his years of selling water softener salts; he lived with his corgi dogs and read paperback thrillers in his graveled back yard. He had a shiny, waxed Subaru but for most errands he used a moped, which coughed and crept slowly under his mass. Jerry Teasdale had become a large man.

Fortunately for Erich, Jerry had friends in Los Angeles who would assist his transition to the west. But first they got acquainted. One night, after polishing off an impressive quantity of meat skewers, Jerry took out old pictures of Erich's father. He'd arranged them in several volumes with handsome cowhide covers. "These photos were in Dan's things when he passed."

Some of the images Erich recognized instantly, publicity stills for "A Touch of Ambrosia." His parents in sequins, waving silk kerchiefs, white doves fluttering from shining pans. Other photos, though, were new to Erich. A black-and-white shot of granddad Lou in his navy uniform, standing beside a lilac bush, his eyes slyly averted. A later photo of his grandparents holding up a squirming Danny Ambrose as a toddler, legs kicking air as if trying to climb into the sky. There was also a shot of a very young Erich with his father in front of a Christmas tree, his mouth open in surprise. The photo was an odd shape, almost triangular, because someone had cropped it with scissors. "I didn't do that," Jerry softly volunteered. (The feet of Erich's mother, though, were still visible.) The effect was lugubrious but the main thing Erich noticed was the resemblance between himself and his father as a toddler in the other photo. The same hairline and cast of mouth. It also occurred to him that he was *older* now than his father had been in any of the adult photos. It didn't seem possible. But here he was, sitting with Jerry Teasdale, plotting the rest of his life. It felt very peculiar.

"We were young and crazy," Jerry said. "But your dad was always serious, too. He made me want to settle down. It's such a shame about the accident. He intended to spend time with you, Erich, to share a life. I know he did."

"Yeah. I guess."

"*Really.* I know I can't put myself in your place. And I wouldn't blame you if you were mad at me."

All was silent, aside from the sound of a corgi dog's toenails on the kitchen tiles as he approached a water bowl.

Jerry pursued, "Are you mad at me?"

"I was," Erich admitted. "But not anymore. It doesn't matter. I don't want to be mad at anyone. It poisons a person."

Jerry smiled. "Oh, you're just like him." He squeezed Erich's hand. "I could never replace him but I always hoped you'd consider me an uncle."

Erich looked at Jerry's round red face. He'd never entertained such a thought. But he supposed it was feasible.

"We're the only ones left," Erich said.

"Well, I hope you're going to share a life with somebody. Aren't you? Turn the page, pal. You can start afresh."

Before long, Erich left Weebanks and drove over the mountains to Los Angeles and, with the help of Jerry's contacts, he got a job delivering and assembling fitness gear. He knew nothing about the job but he was quick to learn, and the deliveries provided a useful crash course in finding his way around the city. He started performing, too. There was more competition in Los Angeles and in the beginning it was hard to get gigs, but he persisted.

The style was edgier here. One local close up artist had created a sensation and gotten media coverage by performing a routine with a torn and restored butterfly. Taking a real insect out of a small cage, he held it by the wings and ripped it in half. This violence always got a gasp out of the audience, sometimes a cry of spontaneous indignation. But then he brought his hands together and suddenly, the butterfly was restored, whole again, and when released from his fingertips, it fluttered away, over the heads of spectators, to their delight.

The first time Erich saw this trick, he was surprised, too, while noting that the rest of the performer's act was standard fare. Mediocre. But, with this stunt, he'd made a hit.

The second time Erich saw this trick, he quickly deciphered the method. For starters, the butterfly was supplemented by a second butterfly, kept out of sight. The first one really *was* torn in half, for the sake of effect; then the appearance of the second one brought a reassuring restoration.

This performance stirred a mixture of disgust and embarrassment in Erich. It was ironic, disagreeably so, to have been fooled by his own grand-dad's trick! Good God. It was an updated, crueler version of the broken and restored cigarette, and it somehow seemed in keeping with the times. The experience led Erich to rethink and sharpen his own act, along opposite lines, with respect to a Somewhere Else grounded on something other than hurt.

Progress came slowly, but by his sixth year in Los Angeles, he felt a quiet confidence, a sense of having remade himself anew. He got regular gigs and reduced his day job to part-time. Twice he enjoyed extended bookings in the close-up gallery at the Magic Castle, which was a top venue. His mother and Brice flew in from Florida, and Jerry Teasdale drove over the mountains from Weebanks, to cheer him on.

Most importantly, by then he'd met Inez. She was his keenest source of happiness. Upon his arrival in the city Erich had alternated periods of trying to meet women and then giving up; it had been a dispiriting social cycle. But one night he'd spoken to Inez Duarte at a party in Topanga Canyon. She'd retreated to the back porch because the music was too loud; Erich had come outside seeking distance from all the drinking inside; and looking at a jagged horizon of darkness and lights, they'd struck up a conversation. Inez had a broad, slow smile, a slight overbite, and Erich liked to see her laugh. She was short and curvy-plump, with long curly hair. Inez was very different from Alison Keating.

Within six months of this encounter on the back porch, they'd moved in together, at a complex near Baldwin Hills where Inez's brother, a weightlifter named Rafael who had melon-sized biceps, had bought and renovated several units. Their place was affordable if they did the restoration work themselves. Inez was a nurse at LAC USC Medical Center, so the location was an easy commute for her.

"Erich, what time will you be home?"

Erich sipped his coffee. "Five o'clock. Six latest."

It was a Saturday morning, and Inez still wore a pair of purple pajama shorts. She'd worked a night shift and her eyes were puffy. Today he'd agreed to perform in a sidewalk show in Santa Monica, a fundraiser for a Christmas food bank. He was working for free alongside other street artists. He hadn't done that sort of open-air busking since the old days by the Roosevelt Road El near Soldier Field, doing his mug and egg routine.

She asked, "Will you bring back the Samoan pearl?"

Erich had promised to repaint the apartment, and they'd looked at a range of color samples. Inez preferred a light shade with darker undertones called "Samoan pearl."

He kissed the top of her head.

"Yes. You'll get your pearl."

On the drive to the gig, Erich felt blessed in every sense. For drinking, he hadn't lapsed; he still talked on the phone to Fred Cunningham at least once a month. Fred had fallen and fractured his shoulder and he was increasingly forgetful, but he'd also reconciled with his daughter and he was in decent spirits. Erich sometimes sent him money to supplement his Social Security. Fred was still Fredding.

Since coming to California, Erich hadn't heard from Agent Heffernan or Doug, and sometimes months passed without his even thinking of them. Of course, he was on the grid and easily traceable; he had no illusions about that fact. But no one had bothered him and he felt that he'd left the room. Someday—soon, he thought—he'd have to sit down with Inez and tell her about this strange chapter from his past.

The fundraiser in Santa Monica was on the 3rd Street Promenade. It was especially crowded on a Saturday, a non-stop stream of shoppers and tourists. Erich was scheduled to follow a juggler on stilts, who performed his stunts while passersby dropped money into an iron bucket marked for the food bank.

The juggler finished his set, and there was a pause while Erich set up his table and unwrapped his gear. "*HEY* everybody!" He launched into a routine with colored credit cards that appeared mysteriously at his fingers. "Just can't get rid of them. Look—there's another one!" The angles weren't easy, in these conditions, but after years of honing and simplifying the routine, his timing was nearly perfect.

But today he got into trouble. It happened when he noticed, among the onlookers, a dark-eyed woman with a piercing gaze. She seemed familiar. She was stern, with silver streaks in her black hair. Then he saw, standing next to her, a blond kid with a pug nose.

And he realized: that's the nanny! From Wilmette, from the terrible birthday party with Mr. Boots! And that kid—yes, it was Viktor. Taller, adolescent now, but undoubtedly, it was the young Plutov.

Do they recognize me? Erich wondered. He scanned the faces in search of Serena, but he didn't spot her.

Erich continued his performance, manipulating the credit cards, painfully conscious of their presence. He fumbled a move that he'd practiced for years, and tried to pass it off as a joke. Hurriedly he transitioned to the next phase of the trick, in which each card turned into a twenty-dollar bill. The nanny and Viktor pressed to the front and now Erich observed another child, much shorter, clutching the nanny's hand. She'd pulled him forward so that he could see. A little scowling kid with a cowlick.

His face—eerily familiar, though Erich was seeing it for the first time— gave him a start as if a camera had flashed behind his eyes. He dropped a bill and it flitted and fluttered on the breeze and came to rest on the ground. Erich interrupted his routine and knelt to pick it up. The kid met his eye.

"You suck," he said.

A distant roar in his head.

For a moment Erich felt he was observing everything from afar. Himself, the child, the crowd. He could've grabbed the boy and shaken him. *What? What?* Instead, he took a deep breath and returned to his trick. He invited the kid to join the act. Grasping his shoulders, he turned him around to face the onlookers. "I'm going to need your help."

Improvising, Erich forced a smile and folded up the bill. He'd positioned the boy directly in front of him and stretched out his arms, with his hands under the boy's chin. With the last fold, he dissembled leaving the cash in one hand while, under the pretext of turning the boy for a better angle, his other hand ditched the money in his waistband. It wasn't a hard move, with the boy conveniently in front of him. His father had used a similar ploy in the old days when Erich had a small walk-on part in "A Touch of Ambrosia."

"Blow on my hand," Erich said.

The boy obeyed, and Erich revealed that the bill had vanished. The surprise on the child's face got a laugh from the audience, and Erich told him to take a bow.

He cut his act short after this trick, and before the nanny and the boys could get away, he gathered up his kit and followed.

"Hey, do you have a minute?"

The nanny and Viktor exchanged glances as he drew nearer. The little brother piped, "Mister, how did you do that?"

"I wonder," Erich said, his gaze lingering on the child. "What's your name?"

"Johnson Hennessy."

"That's quite a name. And where do you live?"

"Up there." He pointed to the hills overlooking the city.

"Can I help you with something?" the nanny asked.

"As a matter of fact, you can."

"Viktor," she said, "give us a minute. Keep an eye on Johnson."

Silently Viktor took his brother by the hand and led him toward a store window with a toy display. Johnson looked back over his shoulder.

"Did you recognize me right away?" Erich asked.

"No. Viktor did. You're the man with the rabbit, right? What do you want?"

"How's Serena?"

"Mrs. Hennessy. She's very well." The nanny's lips formed a firm line.

"I'd like to speak to her."

She shook her head. "You're joking, right? I don't suppose she'll want any more birthday shows, not after the last one."

This woman doesn't know, Erich thought. She has no clue.

He cast another look at Johnson. *Johnson?* God, what a name! His re-semblance seemed obvious, but then again, if you weren't personally con-cerned or didn't know what had happened at that very strange birthday party, maybe it wasn't so obvious. Especially since Serena had moved on, remarried and started a new life.

"It's not about a show," he told her, as the boys returned. Viktor had let go of his brother, who surged toward them, pinwheeling his arms. Antsy to keep moving. "I need to contact her," Erich added.

"Sorry. I can't help you with that."

He could've thrust one of his business cards into her hand, but he doubted she would relay it to Serena. He let them walk away, watching them disappear into the crowd. A saxophone honked behind him, the sound of a snare drum. Another street show was starting.

Well, it couldn't be that hard to find them. He knew their name. He even had an idea of where they lived. As the initial shock wore off, Erich consid-ered the entire shifting world before his eyes, an unpredictable spectacle and the strangest gig of all.

In his gut, he knew that somehow he'd have to pull the situation together: Inez, Serena (well, *Mrs. Hennessy*) and Johnson.

Daunting. Frankly, he would have to perform the impossible.

But as he turned and walked in the other direction, his kit under his arm, he felt he still had time. He was nervous. Yet, in an unaccountable way, he was looking forward to it.

Charles Holdefer grew up in Iowa and is a graduate of the Iowa Writers' Workshop and the Sorbonne. He currently teaches at the University of Poitiers, France.

His short fiction has appeared in many magazines, including *New England Review*, *Chicago Quarterly Review*, *North American Review*, *Los Angeles Review*, *Slice* and *Yellow Silk*. His story "The Raptor" won a Pushcart Prize.

He also writes essays and reviews which have appeared in *The Antioch Review*, *World Literature Today*, *New England Review*, *The Dactyl Review*, *The Collagist*, *l'Oeil du Spectateur*, *New York Journal of Books*, *Journal of the Short Story in English* and elsewhere.

ALSO BY CHARLES HOLDEFER

NOVELS

Back in the Game (2012)
The Contractor (2007)
Nice (2001)
Apology for Big Rod (1997)

STORIES

Magic Even You Can Do: By Blast (2019)
Dick Cheney in Shorts (2017)

CRITICISM

George Saunders' Pastoralia: Bookmarked (2018)